Emily's Destiny

Allan Pritt

Published by New Generation Publishing 2012

Copyright © Allan Pritt 2012

First published in hardcopy in 2009 by Sid Harta
Publishers Pty Ltd
ISBN; 1-921362-01-4 or
EAN13: 978-1-921362-01-9

Published as an eBook in June, 2011 by
ETEXT PRESS Publishing
ISBN: 978-1-921968-01-3

The author asserts the moral right under the Copyright,
Designs and Patents Act 1988 to be identified as the
author of this work.

The book is a work of fiction and all characters in it are
fictitious. Any resemblance to actual persons, living or
dead is purely coincidental.

All Rights reserved. No part of this publication may be
reproduced, stored in a retrieval system or transmitted,
in any form or by any means without the prior consent
of the author, nor be otherwise circulated in any form
of binding or cover other than that which it is published
and without a similar condition being imposed on the
subsequent purchaser.

www.newgeneration-publishing.com

 New Generation **Publishing**

About the Author

A native of Cumbria, Allan was educated at Workington Grammar School and after serving two years National Service, worked for the National Coal Board for eleven years before migrating to Perth, Western Australia.

After working for twenty-eight years in the University of Western Australia Central Administration, he is now retired. Allan is married and they have a grown up family.

Chapter 1

Although I've been in bed for over two hours, I'm still awake. I lie in the dark, listening, waiting.

I hear the key in the lock, the door opening and the first stumbling steps as he enters. Then the thud as the door closes, followed by a second thud as he falls back onto it.

There is a shuffling noise as he staggers up the passage towards the stairs, in the dark. The click of the light switch follows, then the sound of his slow heavy footsteps on each stair, accompanied by his laboured breathing and more cursing.

He pauses on the tiny landing at the top, outside my bedroom door to recover from the ascent.

The click as the light is turned off, then the squeak as he opens the door to their bedroom, opposite mine. I hear his stumbling entry into the room, the thud as he kneels heavily on the floor and the scraping of the chamber pot being dragged from under the bed. The sound of him voiding his bladder of most of his weekly wage; it's Friday night.

More cursing and heavy breathing as he stands up again. Then the clump made by his boots after he removes them and drops them one at a time onto the floor.

The creak of the bed springs, then silence.

His steady breathing, a few loud grunts, then his rhythmic snoring indicates that my mother, lying beside him will be spared my father's unwelcome attention, or a beating if she resists.

It's the signal for me to relax and fall asleep. This is our life. My name is Emily Wilson. I'm ten years old.

**

It's been this way since I was old enough to be disturbed by their nightly noises and moved into the front room.

I often think about my father and the strange relationship we have. We live under the same roof, yet we have no contact with each other. When I was very young I didn't think much about it. There were just the three of us in the house. I thought my mother was there to look after me and my father went to work. But when I grew older, I saw a bit more of him and asked him a few questions, you know general things or about words in my book I couldn't understand. He would ignore me as if I wasn't there.

Although there are other children living in the street I'm not allowed to join in the skipping or hopscotch games they play. My mother considers them rough and ignorant. We never visit anyone, except sometimes my Uncle Arnold and Aunty Iris. I don't get to see how other people live.

I know we are different. I began to realise this when I started school. Other children often call their fathers 'Daddy'. I never do. My mother always refers to him as 'your father' and never 'Daddy'. I see other children being cuddled on their father's knees but I somehow know that this will never happen to me.

When I was five years old I could read quite well. My mother taught me before I started school and I have been in a grade higher than my age since shortly after I started.

'Mother,' I said one day, 'why doesn't my father speak to me or ever read a newspaper or any of your books?'

'Your father doesn't know how to communicate with people very well, especially little girls.'

'Why doesn't he like girls?' I asked. 'Is it because of the baby boy who died before you had me?'

My mother did not answer. She had previously told me that their first child had been a boy but he had only lived a few weeks.

'He shouldn't take it out on me because he lost his son.'

'I'm sure that's not the reason. He doesn't mean to take it out on you. I don't think he could have been much better with a boy. He didn't have a good education. He can't read very well. Remember me showing you the village he grew up in when we passed by it on the bus? Well, all the children in the village, no matter how old they were, sat in the same classroom. The teacher tried to teach them all but, as your father was not very quick at learning, he was left behind the others.'

'Why didn't his parents teach him?'

'They were coalminers and not well educated themselves and his father died when he was very young.'

I accept this explanation but I still have a lot more questions. I love my mother but find her relationship with my father very confusing and can't understand why they are still living together. I know other children at school whose fathers don't live with them.

**

I usually sympathise with Mother when I see her crying in the morning or see fresh bruises, because I know she's had a beating. But this morning I decide I won't. I look at the dark skin around her left eye and shake my head, as she sometimes does to me when she's been annoyed by something I've done.

'If he's so horrible to you all the time, why are we still living with him?' I ask.

'Because I have you to look after, so I can't work. We need the money he earns to live on.' She says.

'Why did you marry someone like him in the first place, I wasn't here then.'

'He wasn't always like this. There was a time when everyone liked him. Certain things happen that we can't control, causing circumstances to change, which make people change. He left school at a difficult time. It was 1926, the year of the General Strike. The mines were closed and most of the country was out of work. When the mine re-opened, his brother wanted him to work with him, underground. Your father wouldn't, so they threw him out of the house. He was only fourteen and had to come to Workington to look for work.'

'Is that when he came to live with you?'

'No, not then. I was still in Oldham. Your Aunt Jane and I were well educated and even though since the Great War, you've heard about that, remember, 1914 to 1918, women were employed in jobs previously closed to them we still couldn't find work in Workington. Anyone who knows Workington would understand this,' Mother continues.

'What do you mean by understanding Workington?' I say.

'I mean understands its history. Get your satchel. You wrote about it at school last year.'

I bring my satchel and take out my notebook.

'Now I remember,' I say, and turn to the page to read out loud what I had written.

The small town on the Cumberland coast is thriving now but was little more than a fishing village until the seventeenth century. The Industrial Revolution attracted iron and steel makers to the area with the discovery of high quality hematite iron-ore. A man called Henry Bessemer introduced a revolutionary steel making process and Workington became the centre of steel production in Northwest England. The Lonsdale Dock was opened in 1865 improving the harbour to allow easier access to shipping for worldwide transportation. By the nineteenth century, if you lived in Workington, you earned your living from steel or coal, so it was a good place to live.

'Now do you see what I mean? But it should read that it was a good place to live if you were a man. And it is not much different now.'

Our mother almost threw us out because she said we were getting under her feet. So, we went to Oldham and worked as upstairs downstairs maids in a big house, for a rich family. Mr and Mrs Oldfield they were called. They owned a cotton mill. They were very kind to us. I liked it there and stayed for four years.'

'Why did you come home if you liked it there?'

'That's what I meant when I said that certain things happen that we can't control. After the Great War other countries started making cotton and making it cheaper than we could, so most of the mills had to close down. The Oldfields' was one of them. They went to live down south. London, I think. Your Aunt Jane had met Uncle Bob by then. They got married and settled in Oldham. He worked in the Oldfields' mill and when he lost his job he started up his own business, cleaning windows. He is doing well, so you could say that his circumstances changed for the better. My mother wasn't well at the time and I came home to look after her.'

'Is that when you met my father?'

'Not long after. But that's enough storytelling for now. You'll wear me out.'

I'm not much wiser for asking. She still hasn't told me why she married him and we never have enough money to live on.

**

Since finding out about his poor education I have tried to like my father but it's difficult, as he does some really mean things to us. On my ninth birthday, in April 1943, my mother took me to Keswick for the day. It is my favourite place. I love the lake and the mountains and as it was spring there were daffodils everywhere. The air is always fresh and clean and the fields surrounding it look like a patchwork quilt and are divided by moss covered dry-stone walls. Yellow and bright is how I always picture Keswick, while Workington where we live is grey and dull. Grey houses and grey streets, made even greyer by the clouds of grey smoke that billow across the sky whenever the blast furnaces at the steelworks are in operation.

'I have a treat for you tonight. I've made a Cumberland tatie-pot for our dinner,' Mother says on the way home. But when we get there, my father has come home from work early and, although it was big enough for the three of us, he has eaten the lot. I can see my mother is annoyed but she doesn't say anything to him. She makes us cheese on toast. I hate cheese on toast.

I try to avoid having to eat at the same time as my father because watching him makes my stomach turn. He has no manners whatsoever. My mother has taught me to eat properly. She says it is important. She tells me about her former employer in Oldham, Mrs Oldfield, telling her children to keep their mouths closed as they chew and to use only their fork to carry food to their mouth.

'Your knife must never touch your mouth' she would tell them.

My father shovels food into his mouth alternately using both knife and fork and chews with his mouth wide open, while making a disgusting noise.

Chapter 2

'You never finished the story of how you met my father,' I say. I have hinted about it a few times lately. For some unknown reason she is avoiding telling me. But I am determined.

'I wasn't home from Oldham long before my mother's health improved and she didn't need me to look after her. But by this time, your Uncle Arnold's wife Iris was having your cousin Margaret, so I spent a lot of my time helping her. Your father had found a job at the coal depot, filling sacks with coal to sell to the deliverers. A nice man called John Watson owned a delivery round and saw how easily your father lifted the heavy sacks. They each weighed one hundredweight and your father threw them about like they were filled with feathers. Mr Watson was getting old, so he got your father to work for him delivering coal. They delivered coal to Arnold's house and that's where I met your father. One day when I was there helping Iris. The Watsons had lost their two sons in the Great War and Mrs Watson took a liking to George, your father, so he went to live with them.'

I try to picture my father throwing heavy things about and can't because of how he looks. He is a huge man, much bigger than most of the other men around and his stomach sticks out beyond his chest and hangs over the waistband of his trousers. Trousers that are held up with string, as none of his belts will go round his waist and he refuses to wear braces. He shows no interest in his personal appearance whatsoever. His arms and shoulders are flabby. He is fast losing his hair. His head is beginning to look like a giant egg. If he has any redeeming features, I can't see them.

'He doesn't look as if he could lift heavy things now. He's too fat.' I say.

'He wasn't in those days. He was much admired for his physique. He was always popular at the pub. He used to show off a bit by beating everyone at arm wrestling, and he was quite the sporting hero on one occasion. Arnold says they still have the ball and a commemorative plaque in a glass case behind the bar of the Railway Hotel.'

'How did you get so friendly with him and what happened to the Watsons? Do they still live in Workington?'

'I first met Mrs Watson at your cousin Margaret's christening. She talked about your father. That's when I found out about his poor education and being turned away by his family. I felt sorry for him and decided to help him. You know, to have a better life. Then Mrs Watson died of a heart attack. Mr Watson took it badly. They had been married for forty years. I took over the running of the business and the house. I always had their dinner ready when they came home after delivering the coal. They were happy times for me, we lived like a family.'

'What happened?'

'Another case of circumstances beyond your control happened. Mr Watson came home one day and said he had lost the desire to carry on anymore without his wife. He sold the business and the house, just like the Oldfields' did in Oldham. He went to live with his sister in Penrith. Your father was very upset. He lost his home and his job all at once. He got a job at the steelworks but had to go back into lodgings, in Moss Bay, which he didn't like.'

'What did you do?'

'I went back to live with my mother.'

**

I hear the letter slot lid being lifted and the sound of someone pulling out the length of string with the key tied to it.

'That'll be your Uncle Arnold, Emily. You go down. I just need to tidy up my hair.'

By the time I get downstairs Uncle Arnold has inserted the key in the lock and is opening the front door.

'Paper man,' he calls out, as he walks up the passage. It has become his habit after reading the previous day's paper to deliver it to my mother, as she cannot afford to buy one for us.

Mother greets him with a smile and I give him a hug as he enters our living room and hands over the paper. I notice that Mother has arranged her hair to cover the latest bruise on her forehead.

'Have you time for a cup of tea?' Mother asks.

'Yes please, my shift doesn't start until one o'clock.' Uncle Arnold is a railway signalman. He often works afternoon shifts.

'I noticed the coalman at the top of the street, Ruth, and it's beginning to rain,' he warns her.

'Oh dear, would you mind Emily,' Mother says, knowing I know what is required.

I have done this many times. I open the cupboard door and extract several old newspapers. I carry them to the front door and begin laying single sheets down, overlapping them so that they cover the linoleum completely, doing this up the passage, through the living room and all the way to the back door. Our little terrace house has no rear exit, its rear wall being shared with a similar terrace house in the next street. So the coal has to be delivered through the house to the coal shed in the back yard, and on wet days the deliveryman will have dirty water dripping off him.

My mother says that having lived near a large city for four years she finds Workington 'very parochial' and looks forward to catching up with news of happenings elsewhere through reading the newspaper.

As we sit sipping our tea and waiting for the coalman, Mother reads out loud an article that tells of the mass-production of motorcars, vacuum cleaners, radios and gramophones, refrigerators and washing machines.

'I haven't seen any of these new-fangled goods in the local shops, Arnold,' she says.

'Neither have I, but I've seen them in Carlisle. We'll have to wait our turn as usual.'

Mother smiles at this. 'You know that such luxuries are well beyond my expectations. I can barely manage to clothe and feed the three of us as it is with what I get of George's wages, before he spends them on beer.'

Once the coalman has departed and Arnold has said his goodbyes, I clear the floor of newspapers and Mother starts on her ironing, filling the air with steam from the damp clothes. She smiles as she once more removes the flatiron from the fire embers.

'I have just recalled reading another article stating that England now has a highly developed national grid of high-voltage electricity transmission lines. Then why am I still ironing with this flatiron and managing with gas lighting. And we can't even afford to buy a gas cooker.' Mother still smiles but she looks tired and there is a dreamy, faraway look in her eyes.

Mother does all her cooking over the open fire and her baking in a small cast iron oven heated by the fire. So, we have to light the fire almost every day, even during summer, which makes the small room stifling hot and the air forever filled with the lingering smell of whatever she's been cooking. Our 'refrigerator' is the cupboard under the staircase. It's the coolest place in the house. The washing is done in a small back room in a deep stone wash trough. Mother fills it with cold water and heats it by lighting another smaller coal fire underneath. Then we squeeze the water out of the clothes and sheets and things between the two large wooden rollers of the cast-iron mangle that stands in the tiny backyard and hang them on the clothes line to finish off.

Mother has often compared our little house with the large one of her former employer, or her parent's family home. She tells me that her only consolation is to keep our home as spotlessly clean as circumstances will allow.

Chapter 3

The only indulgence I have ever known Mother to allow herself is a crystal radio set, and even this she bought through slyly hiding away a few pennies each week. She is always careful to hide it from my father and only listen to it when he is out, as she says she doesn't want to earn herself a few more bruises by giving him a reason to accuse her of wasting money. Concealing it requires a great deal of ingenuity, as the set needs an aerial. Uncle Arnold showed her how to create an aerial by connecting a wire from the radio to an iron bedspring in my bedroom and earthing it through another wire attached to the metal fastening on the window sash.

The reception is not good, but by using the set in my bedroom, we are less likely to be discovered before Mother has the chance to dismantle the arrangement should my father come home unexpectedly. It adds an air of excitement for me through sharing in her secret.

We have had the crystal set for about four years now but I can remember the first broadcast I ever heard. It was one day when she switched it on while I was home from school for lunch. We were just in time to hear Mr Chamberlain, the Prime Minister, announce that England was once more at war with Germany. It didn't mean much to me at the time but it changed all our lives.

**

The introduction of food rationing makes Mother's life more difficult.

'How does the rationing work?' I ask.

'Points are allocated to each food item and each family is allocated a number of points,' she explains. 'It is then up to each family to shop around to try and get food for its allocation. This means I have to roam the whole town as not all shops have food at the same time. And of course when I do find food it still had to be paid for, so being short of money is an added problem, as is your father's huge appetite.'

'Does this mean we will sometimes go without food?

'I hope not,' Mother says. 'I'm determined to see that you and I get a fair share of our rations. That's why I've begun to make our main meal of the day at lunch time while you are home from school and I'm deliberately and gradually leaving less and less for your father to eat in the evening.'

'Is this all there is to eat?' My father says one evening.

'I'm afraid so George. There's not much food in the shops and they keep putting the prices up. I'm doing the best I can with what little money I have,' Mother says and winks at me behind his back.

Her strategy works and the following Friday I witness him throw an extra few shillings on the table.

'Here's some more money, make sure I get more food,' he says.

'I have my extra money now, so all I need is some extra ration coupons,' Mother says. 'Your Uncle Arnold has told me of several families in the neighbourhood who like their beer and cigarettes so much that it takes precedence over food and they send their children knocking on doors clutching handfuls of ration coupons to try and sell for money. I will have to watch out for them.'

'But won't that be like taking food out of the children's mouths?' I say.

'Maybe, and I feel bad at what I'm proposing, but I excuse myself by believing that if I don't buy them someone else will.'

The following Friday evening, being pay day, we sit in the front room in the dark, mindful of the blackout rules, moving the curtain aside every now and then to allow us to peer up the darkened street. We don't have to wait long before two small children walk down the street. We watch them knock on a few doors as they make their way towards our house.

They are turned away from some houses while being successful at others.

With me by her side Mother creeps to the front door, opens it and beckons them.

'Do you want to buy some coupons Missus?' the older looking of the two asks.

He can be no more than eight or nine years old and is holding a younger looking girl with one hand while offering some loose ration coupons to Mother with his other.

Tears fill my eyes at the sight of them. They are shabbily dressed and pitifully thin and have a strong unpleasant body odour. They must be worse off than us, I think.

'Show me what you've got,' Mother says.

Very trustingly he hands her the coupons.

She shows them to me and I see that there is a meat coupon and some clothing coupons still available.

'We're in luck Emily. You need some new shoes, you are growing so quickly,' she says and then her brow furrows. 'I have suddenly realised that I have no idea how much cigarettes cost or how much I should pay for the coupons. I should have asked Arnold.'

'How much do you want for them all?' Mother asks the boy.

The boy shakes his head and gives her a baffled look.

I notice that the girl is carrying a brown paper bag.

'May I see what you have in there?' I ask.

She holds it out to me.

I open it and see a florin, two single shillings, two sixpenny pieces and a few pennies. I show them to Mother. She nods to me and hands the bag back and gives the boy two of the four extra shillings that my father gave her.

'I'd like to give them more but it isn't going to benefit these children and it's all I can afford,' she tells me.

There's a cold wind blowing down the street and I see the children are shivering.

Mother has notice it too.

'Step inside for a minute, I've got something for you,' she says.

There hesitation is only brief and still holding hands they move into the passage.

Mother leaves us to bring two pieces of cake and a glass of milk for each of them. It is quickly demolished. She makes her own bread and cake whenever there is flour and yeast available although the cakes are usually sweetened with honey or apples as there is never any sugar.

There is a plentiful supply of dairy produce in Workington without the need to waste precious coupons. Horse drawn carts from the surrounding farms bring locally grown produce to the door. Some enterprising citizens have taken advantage of the government's 'Dig for Victory' campaign that encourages people to grow their own vegetables by providing garden allotments, and they sell their surplus stock from wheelbarrows on street corners.

I feel better knowing that at least for tonight these children will not go hungry.

'Make sure you come to me first next time,' Mother tells them, 'and I'll make sure you get another treat.'

**

There is a knock on the front door.

'It's seven o'clock at night. Arnold would have used the key. That can only be one other person,' Mother says.

I go down the hall and see that the letterbox lid is lifted and a pair of eyes looking through it.

'I've come to arrest you for showing light through the window. You'll have all the German bombers heading straight for Workington,' a voice calls out.

I open the door. Uncle Alec stands there. He's somewhere around fifty, five foot five or six and slim and wiry. He is not really my uncle but we call him that because he is good friend. He wears a uniform of sorts. An ARP armband, a tin helmet and he carries a small case containing his gas mask. He was considered too old for call up, so he volunteered to be an air raid warden. Not that there are likely to be any air raids. As he explained to me, the steelworks and docks would be prime targets for the German bombers, but Workington is too far north for their limited range. Uncle Alec still acts the part though by patrolling the streets and cautioning any would-be offenders about the blackout rules and encouraging everyone to go to the air raid shelters whenever the siren sounds for the practice drills.

'If you agree to let us off this time, we'll give you a cup of tea,' I tell him.

'It's a deal.' He says, and walks past me into the house.

Mother already has the kettle boiling and greets him with a warm smile. 'Bit nippy out there tonight. I expect you'll need a hot cuppa to keep you going.'

'That'll be lovely Ruth and I'll be glad to take the weight off my feet for a few minutes,' he says.

I go back to reading my book. Or so I want them to think. They seem to forget I'm here when I'm quiet and I hear all sorts of gossip I'm not supposed to.

'So, how are things?' he asks, when he gets his tea.

'You tell me. You probably see more of George than I do,' Mother says.

'Aye, I see him. I usually pop into the pub for a quick one, even when I'm on duty. But it's not the same these days. There's no longer the banter between us. Even the pub's changed. The bartenders have all been called up and the woman who serves there now has grandsons in the forces. Last night there was George and me and two old men playing dominoes, hardly worth being open for.'

'He still goes though,' Mother says.

'Aye, I feel sorry for George in a way. There were always stories of him doing the work of two normal men when he worked at the Rail Bank. You know what I mean, when he had to turn the hot heavy rails by hand to stop them from cambering. People looked up to him then on account of his strength. Now that the steelworks have stopped making rails and are making shell casings and metal sheets for ships and planes and he's in the Loading Bank, all he does is manoeuvre the steel sheets in place on the flat wagons before the cranes release them. And even though they're exempt from call up, on account of the steelworks being classed as an essential wartime service like it is, since most of the men joined up anyhow and are away in the war, those that are left, like, it's like they're not real men. It's like they're not doing their bit. Unless, they're old like me, or sick, like, that is. To make things worse, the steelworks is now hiring women! Imagine George with women working alongside of him. His pride will be dented by that,' Alec tells her.

'Maybe so, but since you're feeling sorry for him, his problems don't stop there,' Mother replies. 'He gets frustrated not knowing what's happening in the war. He can't read a newspaper, never listens to a wireless or crystal set and never goes to the pictures. So he never even sees the newsreel before the movie.'

'You're right. I never thought about that. And with how he is at pub these days he won't hear any of the pub gossip about it either. No one goes near him anymore. I feel bad saying it but even I try to keep out of his way.'

He puts his empty cup down.

'Thanks for that, Ruth,' he says, before turning towards me. 'I'm off now Emily. Goodness knows how many German parachutists have landed on the Cloffocks while I've been sitting here.'

I look up from my book. 'Going already, I hadn't noticed you drinking your tea. I expect the German spies will have spread the word that you're on duty tonight and the planes will stay away.'

He laughs, looking towards my mother and she gets up to see him out.

My book stays in my lap as I sit looking into the fireplace. So, my father has problems due to the war, and Uncle Alec feels sorry for him. Well I don't. Whatever his problems are, they are no reason for him to come home from the pub drunk and take it out on my mother.

Chapter 4

The landlord has just had our house wired for electricity and installed an electric stove, allowing us to switch on the light, cook on a hot plate and not have to light the coal fire in summer. We must be about the last people in the street to get electricity. Most people would find it hard to believe that we could have still been without electricity in 1944!

It's Sunday morning and I'm learning to use the new oven by helping Mother to make a meat loaf. Not that there's to be much meat in it as she says that meat is a luxury we can't always afford.

We hear the sound of someone knocking on the front door.

'Who can that be on a Sunday?' Mother says.

We go together and open the door. A man stands there, a cloth cap in his hand. He's wearing working men's clothes, a blue collarless shirt, dark trousers held up with a broad black belt and boots on his feet.

'Mrs Wilson?' he asks.

'Yes, I am Mrs Wilson,' Mother says.

'Could I have a word with George please? I'm his brother Ted.'

He's much smaller than my father but I can see a likeness in his face. So, this is one of the people who threw my father out. He looks to me as if he's holding himself very stiffly, as if he's feeling tense.

'Then you've had a wasted journey. He's at work,' Mother says. Her voice is stern and I wonder if she's thinking the same as I am.

Ted seems to relax at this news.

'Oh that's too bad. I came on a Sunday because I thought he would be in. Will you give him a message then? Tell him his mother's died and the funeral is on Wednesday. He might like to come.'

'I'm sorry to hear that,' Mother says. 'I will give him the message, but he's hardly likely to attend the funeral. He hasn't seen any of his family since you threw him out of the house.'

The man draws back looking surprised. 'We didn't throw him out of the house. If that's what he told you, it's wrong. He had a choice and it was me that give him it. It had nothing to do with our mother. "Either start earning some money or get out," I said. So he left.'

'Not much of a choice was it. Not everyone wants to work down the mine.'

'You would have had to have been there at the time to appreciate the situation we were in,' Ted argues. 'It was a bad time for us. We were desperate for money. I was the man of the house after our father died. "Pneumoconiosis" they called it, a fancy word for sucking coal dust down his lungs all his life. George's brother Fred was killed in the Great War, so his other brother Frank was the only one working. He'd lost a leg down't pit and was working as a storeman. There was four of us to feed off his wages 'cause I was still out of work following the General Strike. I was better educated than most of the other miners and active in the union, so I had a lot to say during the negotiations. None of us so-called militant miners was re-employed. And it was hard for us to get a job anywhere else. It wasn't for want of trying, you can bet your life on that. I tried really hard, God knows. George had just left school when the pit re-opened. He was only fourteen but he was bigger than most of the grown men in the village. He should have stayed and gone to work.'

'Perhaps saying you threw him out under those circumstances is a bit harsh,' Mother acknowledges. 'I will give him the message but I doubt if he will attend.'

'I don't suppose he will. But I've done what I thought was the right thing, as I always try to do, so the choice is his now,' he says. Then he looks at me. 'You're a fine looking lass. I only wish his mother could have seen you. She always worried about him, up 'til the day she died.'

I didn't know what to say. He seems to be a nice man and looks as if he's about to cry. He nods to my mother, puts his cap on and walks away.

Mother closes the door.

'He seems to be a nice man. He's as much my uncle as Uncle Arnold isn't he? Fancy us having a family we've never met. That Mrs Watson can't have known the full story either,' I say.

'It sounds like none of us did. We only ever knew what your father told us. And we are not likely to meet his family now.'

**

Of course having electricity means having to have a ready supply of pennies with which to feed the meter. So we keep a glass jar full on the mantelpiece in the front room, where the meter is.

One evening while my father is at the pub, my mother and I are sitting reading when the lights go out.

'Oh dear!' Mother says. 'I meant to put in some pennies earlier, but I forgot.'

We grope our way in the dark to the front room, but when I pick up the jar it is empty.

'No need to guess where the pennies have gone,' Mother says. 'It was full, so that will have bought him a few pints.' She looks in her purse, but there are no pennies, so we have no choice but to go to bed.

Much later, I hear the sound of my father stumbling and cursing his way to bed, in the dark. I hear him yelling.

'You bloody useless woman, why can't you remember to put pennies in the meter?'

The sound of his fists on her body follows.

Shortly after, I hear his loud snoring and my mother comes into my room. She is whimpering and crying and we lie with our arms around each other until we fall asleep.

I hide my fear as best I can whenever he hits my mother and try not to think about him ever hitting me. I have no real reason to consider this possibility, I tell myself. Sometimes, I feel I'm invisible; he pays me so little attention.

I am usually in bed when my father comes home from the pub, but one evening he comes home early and mother and I are still up reading. I would normally close my book, say goodnight to my mother and go up to my room. But this night I am still so angry at the way he blamed her for not feeding the meter the other night that I continue to read.

Mother looks at me and nods towards the door, indicating that I should leave the room. I ignore her for once and sit staring at my father. He has settled himself on one of the kitchen chairs, at the table. He stares back at me. I can tell he is uncomfortable by my little show of defiance, because he lays both his hands flat on the table and continues to stare at me.

Mother says, 'Emily,' in a stern voice.

'In a minute, Mother,' I reply.

It is then I get scared. My father stands up so quickly that his chair topples over behind him. It is an act of madness, I know, but all I do is close my book and stare at him. He thumps the table before moving round it towards me, his big fists clenched. I know I've been silly and reckless and think I am about to die. Mother moves quickly between us, a large pair of scissors she has been using to cut some material with a short time ago, clearly visible in her hand.

'That would be going too far, George,' Mother says calmly.

He looks her in the eye, then at the scissors, but before either of them can react any further, I say, 'Goodnight Mother,' and leave the room, controlling the urge to run.

Later on, I hear the sound of his fists on my mother's body again and know she is paying for my act of stupidity. She doesn't come to my room this time and I feel ashamed of my actions. I wonder what would happen if I annoyed him again and mother wasn't around? It wouldn't take much of a blow to do me a lot of damage. How long can we continue like this?

Chapter 5

The next big challenge for me is later this year when I have to sit for the Eleven Plus exam. The results of this will determine where I do my secondary education. I'm confident I will do well enough to qualify for the grammar school. I'm at the top of my class in most subjects. I want to do well to please my mother. She's put up with a lot for my sake.

I know there are a few extra problems if I go to the Grammar School. Expensive books to buy and a smart navy blue blazer emblazoned with the school badge. I have asked about the price of a blazer. Mother won't be able to save that much out of what my father gives her, no matter how frugal she is. I mention this to her and say that I don't really mind if I can't go to the grammar school. She tells me not to be silly, that a good education will give me the best chance of a good life and I have to stop worrying about money and concentrate on my studies.

The only way to get money, she says, is to earn it. She says she will have to find a job with hours that allow her to start after my father leaves for work, yet give her time to prepare his evening meal. She says, if my father finds out she is earning money, he will either stop the housekeeping money altogether or reduce what he gives her.

She shows me an advertisement in the local *Star* newspaper. It seems to be too good to be true.

'Domestic help wanted, light duties, and must be honest, reliable and experienced.'

The address is that of a large house in Portland Square.

She tells me she will go and see about it. I am nervous all morning and the time seems to drag as I wait for lunchtime to arrive and give me the opportunity to rush home and hear what has happened.

She is still in her best dress and sitting at the table when I get there. She looks calm

I try to be calm too in case she hasn't got the job. I don't want to add to the disappointment I know she will be feeling if she has missed out.

I raise my head as if sniffing the air as I enter. 'Leek and potato soup, smells delicious,' I say, not really being clever, as I saw the leek and the peeled potatoes on the draining board before I left for school this morning. I go and wash my hands.

'How was your morning at school?' she asks, with a cheeky grin on her face. Mother is not good at pretending.

The grin gives her away. 'You got the job,' I say. 'I want to hear all about it.'

'And so you shall,' she says. 'From the moment I rang the doorbell, I knew the job was for me. You know how I've always admired that beautiful cobblestone square? Well, the house is a three-storey one and it's on one corner of that square. It's quite an imposing house. It really stands out, far and away the best house overlooking the square. Everything about the house is impressive, even the front door. A young woman who looked to be no more than eighteen and who was obviously dressed to go out opened it almost immediately when I rang.

'"My name is Ruth Wilson and I've come to enquire about the domestic help position," I said.

'Then, the snooty little madam says, "Wait there," and calls over her shoulder, "Mother, there's a person here to see about the servant position." A person, indeed! Then, without waiting for a reply, she sets off past me across the square.

'A few moments later a tall handsome-looking woman of about forty appears. "Children! They can be so rude at times. Please come in," she says.

'I follow her through the hallway and down a passage that leads to a large living room. It's a beautiful home with thick pile carpet and expensive furnishings. It reminds me very much of the Oldfield's house. The woman sits down and gestures for me to do the same.

'"Have you worked as a domestic previously?" she asks.

'"Yes, I have," I say. "I was a maid in a large house in Oldham for four years, very similar to this one and I have a reference from my previous employer, a Mrs Oldfield."

'Then she really floors me. "My goodness, you must be one of the sisters. I went to school with Dorothy Oldfield. She said that one of you had returned to Workington when I met up with her in Hampshire recently and I told her we had moved up here. She spoke very highly of you," she says.'

'What a coincidence!' I say. 'Go on, Mother.'

'What a coincidence indeed! We spent the next hour or so discussing how remarkable it was over a cup of tea. The woman introduced herself as Mrs Morgan, and said they own that furniture shop in Oxford Street and another one in Whitehaven and her husband divides his time between the two.

'I told her I was married and had a daughter, and explained the reason for wanting work as having time on my hands now that my daughter is at an age where she needs less attention. I was offered the job with hours fixed between eight thirty, after Mr Morgan leaves for work, and eleven thirty. This suits us very well.'

'It sounds as if your luck is about to change. You've found a job and perhaps a friend at the same time,' I tell her.

Chapter 6

It's Saturday morning and I call at Uncle Arnold's house to collect the paper. He has chores to do on Saturdays and as I have no school it saves him having to deliver it to us. My cousin Margaret opens their front door just as I am about to knock.

'Hi Emily, go on in. I'm just on my way to the shops,' she says, and sets off up the street.

I enter and before I have chance to call out and let them know I have arrived, I hear Uncle Arnold's voice.

'You should see our Ruth's arm, it's black and blue and just about hanging off her shoulder,' he says.

'Did you say anything to her?' Aunt Iris replies.

I remain standing in the vestibule and quietly close the door behind me. I know I shouldn't eavesdrop but excuse my bad manners this time because they are talking about my mother.

'Wouldn't dare, she would simply tell me to mind my own business again.'

'I wonder what's supposed to have caused it this time. She can't keep forever saying her bruises are from falling down or bumping into doors,' Iris says.

'Probably happened on Wednesday night. George was in a foul mood when he left the pub. Remember me telling you that the place was full of uniforms, even though the war in Europe has only been over for a few weeks. They were throwing a party for the homecoming of two of the pub stalwarts, Nobby Clarke and little Peter Kent. It was quite an occasion. The main bar walls were covered with Union Jacks, and although there was no one playing the piano, the walls seemed to be shaking and the noise was deafening with the singing. Talk about spontaneous. No sooner did one chorus of, *Land of Hope and Glory* finish than someone else would start up with, *It's a Long Way to Tipperary* or that Vera Lynn favourite, *We'll Meet Again*, and everyone joined in. Mind you, the drinks were free so you could call them patriotic fuelled renditions,' Arnold's voice continues.

'I don't understand why having free drinks all night would put George in a foul mood. If it was a Wednesday night as you said, he wouldn't have had much money left, so he would have been expecting a quiet night,' Iris says.

'Aye, but the free drinks and fags were to welcome home little Peter Kent. George would have been thinking back to the time before the war when he was the hero, when it was him that was always the centre of attention. Little Peter Kent and the like used to stand around in the corners drinking their halves of mild and saying nowt to nobody. That's what would have upset George. Also, they were making a big fuss about Peter Kent being a sergeant.'

'A sergeant! Little Peter Kent?' Iris's voice took on an incredulous tone. 'I can hardly believe it. He was a clerk in the steelworks offices before the war and I know for a fact that the only time his wife would let him go to the pub was on a Sunday night because that was the only way she could get him to agree to go to the church with her beforehand.'

'That's just it, isn't it? He was a clerk, and a good one and I happen to know that that's what got him into the Royal Army Pay Corps. He may have been a sergeant but he was no homecoming hero. He served out the war in the army barracks in Aldershot, preparing payments for the active soldiers. Probably can't tell one end of a rifle from the other,' Arnold says.

'So you reckon George would've gone home and taken out his frustration on poor Ruth.'

'I would bet on it Iris. There was plenty of *esprit de corps* about that night but it would have past George by. I watched him. From a distance, mind you. I've seen that wild look come into his eyes once or twice before, when he's taken offence at some remark someone in the bar's made. He's not fussy who cops it when he gets like that. It's usually whoever's nearest. He didn't mind drinking the free beer, mind you. He had more than his share.'

I have heard enough. I knew the night they were referring to only too well. I re-open and then noisily shut the front door.

'Hello, anyone at home? It's your favourite niece,' I call out.

**

Although I had heard the sound of the beating, I am still shocked at the sight of the bruises on my mother's body the next morning. She comes into my room once my father has left for work and slumps onto my bed. Her right arm is hanging limply by her side and she's gritting her teeth as if the pain's too much to bear.

'You can't keep letting this happen, Mother. He's getting worse. You have to report him to the police. Now would be a perfect time, with your arm like this and those bruises,' I tell her.

'I know you're right, Emily, but it's not as simple as that. It might only make matters worse. You don't know him like I do. Your father is like a child in some ways. He needs attention. He craves respect. He had all that once. He was a sporting hero in the pub and was admired at work. Now, because of the war, it's all gone. I honestly don't know what he would do if I reported him to the police. I know he would see it as me shaming him in public and he would never forgive me for that. I have your safety to consider as well as my own. The police can only do so much to protect us. They can't be here all the time. I couldn't look after you if I was maimed or dead and that could easily happen if I made things worse. When he gets in those drunken rages he's uncontrollable.'

It's obvious she will not be able to go to work this day. She asks me to ride my bike to the Morgan's house to let them know, and to say she fell and bruised her arm, and will not be available for the rest of the week.

Chapter 7

I cycle to the Morgan's house as I am bid; but my mind is not on my errand. I know we can't carry on like this. My mother has given me her excuses but my father's behaviour is getting worse. One of these days he will do some permanent damage to her or even kill her, or us both. Our situation has gone from hard to bear to unbearable.

I also realise that while we have to rely on him to provide for us, we will always be poor. I have watched my mother's daily struggle simply to survive. How would I survive without her?

My mother has often told me that she believes in fate, that everyone's destiny is pre-planned, with certain events occurring in their lives that direct them on to the next stage of their journey to their ultimate destination. I don't dispute this, but I also believe that occasionally fate needs a helping hand.

I've made up my mind. We are going to survive and I'm determined to lift our status in life, whatever it takes.

I think for a long time about what I'm about to do. I don't consult Mother beforehand. She will never understand. It's not an easy decision for an adult, let alone a child of eleven.

Or perhaps it's easier for me because I can only see with a child's eye view. Someone's done wrong, so they've got to be punished. My father has hurt my mother. It's wrong for him to do this. I feel no guilt. I've made my decision. Under the circumstances it is the only decision that will give us a chance for a future as opposed to a life of poverty and hopelessness. It's our lives or his. I have spent the better part of my short life listening to news of death, listening to the daily news of men, good men, dying for a good cause. I have simply decided to add one bad man to the list.

**

I hear the key in the lock, the door opening and the first stumbling steps as my father enters. Then the thud as the door closes, followed by a second thud as he falls back onto it.

There is a shuffling noise as he staggers up the passage towards the stairs, in the dark. The click of the light switch follows, but no light. I hear more clicking, more cursing but still no light.

I have earlier removed the light globe.

There's the sound of his slow heavy footsteps on each stair, accompanied by his laboured breathing and more cursing.

I stand on the landing with my back to the wall, knees bent and hands behind me firmly on it. My eyes are accustomed to the darkness. I have been here for an hour.

He's almost reached the top and I can see him, almost feel his short, quick breath. It's Friday night and he'll have had a lot to drink.

One foot appears on the landing and as the other rises his outstretched arms reach forward in search of the doorframes on each side of the narrow landing, to pull himself up.

The moment I see him teeter on the edge of the top step is the moment I have been waiting for. I thrust myself forward, using both hands and one foot against the wall to boost my momentum.

My head strikes his groin with considerable force. The impact knocks me dizzy and I fall back onto the floor.

He involuntarily drops his arms and reaches for his groin and stands poised on the edge of the landing.

For a brief moment it looks as though he will recover his balance, then, as if in slow motion, he begins to fall backwards.

There is a sickening thud as his head hits the stairs. I lose sight of him as he tumbles to the bottom.

Minutes go by, in complete silence. It is broken by my mother's voice.

'Emily,' then much louder. 'Emily!'

'I'm all right, Mother. Wait until I put the light on.'

I bring a chair from my room and stand on it to replace the light globe. Then I put the chair back and switch on the light.

He lies at the foot of the stairs, his head at an odd angle to his body.

Mother comes out of her room and I point to his body.

'He's fallen down the stairs,' I say quietly.

She goes down and puts her hand on his neck.

'I can't find a pulse. I think his neck is broken,' she says.

'Yes mother, I think it might be. I think things are going to be better for us from now on.'

Chapter 8

There is a coroner's inquest, which records a verdict of accidental death. At least a dozen witnesses attest to my father's excessive drinking on the night in question. My mother confirms that the light on the stairs was working; she says she heard her daughter's door opening before she switched it on, after the fall. When asked, we can offer no reason why he should choose to climb the stairs in the dark.

Mother and I never talk about it afterwards. I notice her looking at me rather intently during the inquest and she holds my hand throughout. There are tears in her eyes but none in mine.

If she does have any suspicion that I am hiding something, the nearest she gets to asking is during one evening about a month later. We are sitting quietly reading, when, and it is almost as if she is thinking out loud, she says, 'I have almost no recollection of the night your father died.' That is all she says and goes back to reading her book. I think about it later and decide that it is her way of telling me that she would prefer not to know if I caused his death, but that if I had it was all right with her.

**

Things *are* better for us. Uncle Alec calls round on the Sunday to offer his condolences and brings with him an amount of money he has collected from the pub patrons on Saturday night. This proves to be enough to cover the cost of a funeral, with sufficient left over to put aside for my schoolbooks.

My mother goes to work as usual on the Monday. She tells me later that she astounded Mrs Morgan half way through the morning, by telling her that her husband had died the previous Friday evening following an accident. Mrs Morgan had insisted that she go home, so mother said she confessed to her marriage being a failure and told her that the purchase of a blazer was the real reason she'd had to seek work.

'Well, you can stop worrying about a blazer,' Mrs Morgan had said. 'I believe you met my daughter briefly the first day you came here, while she was home on holiday from University. She attended Workington Grammar School for two years when we first moved here four years ago. We still have her blazer and it's as good as new. I saw your daughter when she brought the news of your accident and she looked about the same size as Patricia was then, so you can have it. That is, if your daughter won't mind wearing a second-hand one?'

'Of course she won't,' Mother had said. 'It's very kind of you to make the offer. There is one more thing though before I can accept it.'

'What's that?' Mrs Morgan had asked.

'Emily will have to pass the exam first.'

Chapter 9

There was only a small gathering at my father's funeral. If, as my mother said, he had once been popular, he was not at the end or his friends' allegiance to him had ceased after they had contributed to his collection at the pub.

I notice a stranger there and as we walk away I say, 'Who's that man, Mother?'

She follows my gaze but seems unsure who it is.

'Why, it's Mr Watson. I hardly recognised him. He must be in his seventies now,' she eventually says.

We catch up with him.

'Mr Watson, how nice to see you again,' Mother says.

'Hello Ruth, you are looking well under the circumstances. I saw the death notice in the *Star* and decided to pay my respects. He was like a son to me as you well know and it hurt me to have to sell the business and put him out of a job.'

'That was a sad time for all of us but we all had to get on with our lives as best we could. It seems so long ago now. I had a visit from George's brother. He told a slightly different story about George leaving home than the one we knew. You remember what it was like at the time of the General Strike of course and it seems the Wilsons had only one breadwinner to keep four of them. They desperately needed money like everyone else and George was given the option of going to work down the mine or to get out. He chose to leave his family and come to Workington. They didn't exactly throw him out. We may have judged the Wilsons too harshly,' Mother says.

He nods his acknowledgement.

'Maybe so, but then again they may have been the ones making the harsh judgement. Perhaps they weren't aware of his fear of the mine. George told me that when he was only seven years old, his father took him for a visit down the mine. It must have left a lasting impression on him. He talked about the cage going down being as black as the coal, the long walk to the coalface with the roof getting lower and lower, the dust and the damp and the fear of the roof falling in as it did when his brother lost his leg. He had knelt where his brother and father worked and said the roof was only a few feet above his head. He told me that he would never go down the pit again. Because of his size and his aggressive nature everyone considered he was afraid of nothing, but he was afraid of the mine. He wouldn't have admitted that to his family.'

'No, I don't suppose he would. We only ever judge by what we can see,' Mother says.

Mr Watson appears to notice me for the first time.

'And who's this pretty girl?' He asks.

Mother opens her mouth to speak but I speak for myself.

'My name is Emily Wilson; I'm pleased to meet you, Mr Watson. My mother has told me about the happy times you shared.'

'And I'm glad I've had this opportunity to meet you, despite the sombre occasion.'

He turns to my mother.

'You must be very proud of her, Ruth. And it was nice to see you again, but I must be on my way. My train leaves in about thirty minutes.'

'Goodbye then, Mr Watson,' Mother and I say in unison and she looks very sad as she adds, 'Take care.'

Chapter 10

Aunt Jane has come to the funeral, giving me the opportunity to get to know her better. Mother and Aunt Jane have corresponded regularly but I have only met her during her two brief visits to Workington when she stayed with Uncle Arnold and Aunt Iris. She is two years older than her sister and I compare the two. Jane is two inches taller and carries herself with an erect posture; she oozes confidence and makes her cheap clothes look good. Mother on the other hand is a shy person and never comfortable with her appearance.

On the day after the funeral I manage to get Aunt Jane alone.

'I know you didn't like my father and it doesn't seem so important now that he's gone, but why did she ever come to marry someone like him?' I ask.

'I'm not surprised to find out that she hasn't told you. I think she realised soon after that she had made a mistake. I honestly don't know the whole story. I met him briefly at your cousin Margaret's christening. I suggested he might be a bit simple and she defended him by telling me he was just uneducated and that his family had thrown him out because he refused to work down the pit. I realised then that she had taken an interest in him, so I didn't say any more. I didn't hear from her for a while and then I got a letter to say they were getting married.

'That's when we fell out with our mother. She didn't approve of Ruth marrying George. She said he was nothing but a drunken lout. Even though I agreed with her I took my sister's side. We had a row with our mother and haven't spoken to her since. Their first baby only lived for a few weeks. Your mother was very sick afterwards and I came to look after her. Your father took it badly. Arnold said he had made a big show at the pub about the child being a boy and saying only real men father boys. Then, when the child died, he went from being the father of a baby son, a man to be admired, to being the father of a dead child and the husband of a sick wife, a man to be pitied. He couldn't handle it. He started drinking more and ignoring his friends.

'It was a couple of months before your mother recovered enough to allow me to go home. During the time I was there I got to see what a good for nothing your father really was.

'He was very mean with his money for a start. The first day I was there, he handed me a pound note, saying that it was for the housekeeping. Your mother was too soft with him. I told him that there were now four of us to feed as well as medicine to buy for your mother and demanded more. That was when I realised he couldn't count.

'He went red in the face, grabbed some money out of his pocket and banged it down on the table. "That's all you're getting so you'll have to make it do," he said.

'I couldn't believe my eyes. There was another pound note and a few shillings lying there.

'Hoping my face wasn't betraying my astonishment I said, "All right I will," and he stormed out of the house. I got that much off him every week I was there after that.

'I didn't have it all my own way though. I moved your mother into the front bedroom, the one you have now, and I slept alongside her. I kept the little coal fire in there burning all the time. It was freezing cold outside.

'Anyway, on the third day he had their bedroom to himself, I met him going down the stairs to work.

'"Piss-pot's full," he says.

'"You filled it you can empty it," I told him.

'He looked as if he was going to hit me but by then he knew I was made of sterner stuff than your mother, so he must have thought better of it.

'The next day I did some washing. It wasn't freezing, so I thought it might dry. I opened the back door to use the mangle and the stench hit me. I looked up at his bedroom window and realised he had emptied the pot out of it into the backyard. I had to swill it away before I could go out there.

'I tried to persuade her to leave him and come to Oldham to start a new life. But she wouldn't. I think her pride got in the way. She didn't want to be a burden on Bob and me, as if she ever would be. Bob thinks the world of her.

'Next thing you turned up. You were her life after that. She was prepared to put up with George and the hovel you lived in as long as you were all right.'

'Thank you for telling me that,' I say.

Chapter 11

As always, I give my mother no reason to be concerned and pass the Eleven Plus exam with ease.

We are much happier now, although we are no better off financially. And while I am left to concentrate on my schoolwork, my mother still struggles with food rationing, even though the war has ended. She says it takes time for a country to recover from a war and tells me to be patient.

Mother reminds me that this is the second world war that she's lived through. She says things are much better in England now than they were after the first war when she was a child.

The first post-war elections end in a win for the Labour Government lead by Prime Minister Attlee, and Nationalisation begins, with the coal industry and the railways coming under government control.

A *National Insurance Act* and a *National Health Act* are passed, giving free medical treatment for all.

We keep abreast of the latest developments and spend our leisure time with our books and our radio, which we enjoy, but apart from Uncle Arnold, Aunt Iris and Mrs Morgan, we have no one else here to call friends.

One day Mrs Morgan pays us an unexpected visit and embarrasses Mother by having her husband deliver us some new furniture the following week. She says it has been in stock for a long time and they have to get rid of it to make way for new stock. I suspect this isn't true and that she feels sorry for us after seeing our old leather sofa, with the holes in the arms and the horsehair stuffing sticking out.

I also believe my mother is embarrassed at not being able to provide better facilities than an outside toilet and a tin bath for me, now that I am growing up and used to indoor plumbing at school. It doesn't bother me. We have the house to ourselves now and bring the bath into the family room in front of the fire when it is cold. Mother is slightly built and has aged well and I have never been shy in front of her.

The *Housing Act* of 1949 introduces subsidies to landlords to improve rented property, but despite this, the houses in our street are showing signs of neglect, and there are now several derelict buildings at the end where we live. It is very depressing.

**

We begin spending a few weeks each year with Aunt Jane in Oldham and on one visit I overhear my mother telling her sister that she is delighted by the bond that has developed between Uncle Bob and me, as she had feared my life with my father might have tainted my opinion of men.

She need not have worried. I also like my Uncle Arnold but have little in common with my cousins, and so I don't spend much time in his company.

I receive my School Leaving Certificate in 1950, the year of my sixteenth birthday. I have developed a love of books and have decided to become a librarian and the Certificate is important to achieving this goal.

Aunt Jane and Uncle Bob attend my graduation, and upon seeing the dilapidated state of my old sit-up-and-beg type bicycle, buy me a brand new one, a Hercules Kestrel, complete with drop down handlebars and three gears.

I know I will have to continue as a student for a while longer in order to become a librarian but I have had enough of studying for the time being. I want to find a job and gain some experience of the adult world. Mother is not convinced that this is a good idea, but we finally agree on the understanding that if I have not found suitable employment within six months, I will begin studying. We never actually define what will be considered suitable employment, but for the time being I am free from studying and I am determined to make the most of it.

Chapter 12

This is worth waiting for, I think, as I cycle my way through Cockermouth. April has arrived and with it some fine spring weather. I was looking forward to exploring the Lake District on my new bike, but the winter was harsh and I've had to bide my time. Time I killed with an extended visit to Aunt Jane's. They are both members of the Salvation Army so I sing alongside Auntie Jane with the Salvation Army choir at a few concerts, with Uncle Bob accompanying us on his cornet in the band and I help Uncle Bob clean windows to pay for my keep.

Now, although there are only three months left in which to find a job, on the warmest day since last October I put all thoughts of work and studies aside and set off on my bike for Keswick, after assuring my mother that if the weather changes I will come home on the train.

It is twenty-one miles from Workington to Keswick and there are plenty of hills in between and as I haven't been able to do any serious cycling for months I take plenty of breaks. With my calf muscles tightening with every turn of the pedals after only eight miles, I stop to look around Cockermouth and the house where William Wordsworth was born. Another ten miles on I sit for a while to look across Bassenthwaite Lake. I am always taken aback by the magnificence of the Lake District landscape. I continue my journey along a narrow main road that is bordered by dry stone walls, retaining slopes of rich pasture with sheep or cows grazing incuriously in some of them. I reach Keswick just after noon. On such a lovely spring day it is difficult to imagine a more picturesque place. In every direction there are beautiful views of mountains and fells, dominated by Skiddaw to the north, its peak covered in snow and the lake, Derwentwater, to the southwest. I have followed the A66 from Workington, so I enter Main Street at its widest and use the extra space to wander around before reaching the part where the street is divided by the Moot Hall with its famous one-handed clock, to make my way down to the lake. Having eaten the sandwiches my mother made for me, I buy an apple and eat it as I stroll along. Even the shops appear pretty. But the fine day has attracted people outdoors and the pavements are crowded. As I approach the lake the streets get even narrower, making it awkward to get near the windows while pushing my bike.

I spot a bookshop. *The Old Book Shop* it is called, and a sign reads, *Books old and new, please come inside and browse*. It really is old looking, with lots of small thick glass windows in place of the usual large panes. I peer through the door and see that the sign *has* attracted some browsers. I also notice two hand-printed signs, *Room to let, enquire within* and *Shop assistant required, enquire within*.

I stare at the signs, all sorts of strange thoughts going through my mind. I have often teased my mother about her belief in fate guiding our paths, but all of a sudden it doesn't seem so unbelievable. Then my face breaks into a smile, I am being silly.

However, my curiosity is aroused and I want to look at the books anyhow, so when most of the browsers come out I prop my bike against an adjacent wall and go inside.

It is larger than it looks from outside and the walls are a mass of book-filled shelves, reaching so high as to require the use of a ladder to reach the top ones. There appears to be only one assistant, a woman about thirty and obviously pregnant.

There are still two browsers in the shop and the assistant looks up and says, 'Do you need any help miss?'

'Not with books, thank you. I'm here to ask about the room,' I say, deciding to ask about the room first.

'Ah! You will need to talk to the owner, Mr Peel, about that. He should be back from lunch very shortly. You are welcome to browse until he returns.'

It's only a matter of minutes before a tall slimly built young man in a dogtooth-patterned sports jacket and dark slacks enters.

'This young lady is here to enquire about the room John,' the assistant tells him.

He turns to me and smiles.

'Hello! My name is John Peel. You may have heard of me.' He speaks with a slight stammer.

'Hello! My name is Emily Wilson. I have heard of you but I thought you would have been much older,' I reply, guessing he is referring to the famous huntsman and going along with the joke.

'Can you manage another ten minutes or so, Sarah, while I show Miss Wilson the room?' he says, addressing the assistant. She tells him she can and he asks me to follow him. He sets off towards the rear of the shop and pulls open a door. It is so skilfully painted to make it blend in with the adjoining bookshelves that I hadn't realised it was there.

'Fools everyone the first time,' he says over his shoulder, anticipating it will have fooled me. Through this door, another, with a narrow flight of stairs on the right, confronts us. I think it must lead to a backyard but when he opens it, I see it is a room containing a small freestanding bath with little claw-like feet at each corner, a white sink and a lavatory. He continues up the stairs to a room directly above the shop.

'The lavatory is shared with the staff during opening hours,' he says, as we stand side by side. Then with a wave of an arm, 'And this is the rest of it.'

The room is quite large and contains a single bed, a two-seater settee, and a small folded dining table with two chairs. There is a large rug over a polished wood floor, and three large paintings on the floral pattern papered walls. *Friars Crag* on one and what appears to be the view from *Surprise View* on another; while the third is of a group of red-coated huntsmen outside an Inn, drinking the stirrup cup.

John Peel walks across the room and pulls back a heavy curtain to reveal a small gas cooker, with three burners on top and an oven underneath them. A small row of pots and pans hangs above it.

'I can vouch for it being practical and comfortable, as I lived in it myself until I got married and it's been empty ever since. It seemed such a waste that I decided to let it. My father added the plumbing downstairs to give me somewhere cheap to live when I first left home.'

I'm very impressed, but what am I going to tell him? I can't say I've only come in out of curiosity. He pulls the two chairs away from the table and indicates for me to sit on one, while he takes the other. I see that he's older than I first thought and guess he's in his late twenties, rather than early. Although his face is long and thin, his features are regular and his longish hair is thick and wavy. I consider him good looking. He has a serious air about him, like a schoolmaster or a clergyman. When he speaks again, I notice his stammer has disappeared.

'Now then, Miss Wilson, are you seriously interested in the room, or just curious?'

Can he read my mind? I decide to bluff it out. 'That depends, because I'm also interested in the job.'

'Is that so? Would you mind telling me how old you are?'

'I'll be seventeen at the end of this month.'

'Then you probably haven't worked before.'

I feel obliged to tell him the whole story, about my School Certificate, my ambition to be a librarian, and wanting a spell from study for a while. I add that I live in Workington with my widowed mother and tell him how much I love Keswick.

'Thank you for being so forthright,' he says. He even talks scholarly. 'I'll be the same. Sarah, my assistant, is leaving in a few weeks to have her baby and won't be coming back. We thought we had a suitable replacement, but she quit after only two weeks, and I was pleased she did, because she wasn't very confident dealing with customers. Sarah is actually the first assistant we've had who's stayed longer than twelve months. By "we", I refer to my father and me. He's now passed away and left the shop to me. He was also a John Peel, but our genealogy research indicates we are not relatives of the famous huntsman. You seem very mature for your age. If I were to offer you the job and the room, would you consider it?'

I listen very carefully and quickly decide. I want them both.

'I love books Mr Peel and the work fits in so well with my plans to be a librarian that I don't see how my mother could object. The accommodation is perfect, but would the wages pay for the rent and leave enough over to feed me?'

He smiles at this. He smiles a lot, and so I consider him to be a happy man.

'Well, you're very young and you've no work experience, but you have a confident air about you, so I'm prepared to take a chance. I'll tell you what I'm prepared to offer and you can go home and talk it over with your mother. The room has been earning nothing for two years, so if it's to be the means by which I get a reliable assistant I'll ask only a peppercorn rent for it. I could start you on, say, fifteen shillings a week, on a trial basis, for, say, three months, the remainder of the time you agreed with your mother. If you want to stay on longer and I'm satisfied with your performance you can.'

I sit in a daze. A job and a home in Keswick! Surely it can't be that easy. There has to be a 'but' in there somewhere.

Suddenly John Peel leaps to his feet, and I think he has remembered something that would make it all impossible, but all he says is, 'Sarah! I forgot about her. She has a doctor's appointment this afternoon and I said she could leave early. Let's continue this downstairs.'

After Sarah has gone, he continues, 'Do you consider yourself old enough, and capable of living on your own?'

'Yes, I'll be fine. I've always helped my mother with the household chores and I did well in the Domestic Science course at school, so I won't starve. If there's nothing else, I'll go home and break the news to my mother. It's almost four o'clock.'

'Yes it is, and if that's your bicycle outside, it's far too late for you to cycle home. I would feel better if you would catch the four thirty train. I'll give you the fare and please phone me with your decision by the end of the week.'

'You have used a telephone I suppose?' he asks as I walk out of the door.

'Oh yes,' I assure him, but don't consider it necessary to mention that the first time was on my

Uncle Bob's recently installed one, only a few months ago.

I put my bike in the guard's van. This late afternoon train is always busy as it starts from Penrith, which is on the main Scotland to London line and is a connecting train for travellers coming to the west coast. As it hisses and puffs its way to Workington, I sit in the crowded carriage mulling over the situation, oblivious to the beautiful scenery sliding by the window and the conversations going on around me. Have I been too hasty? Do I really want this job? Do I really want to leave home and live on my own? Can I leave my mother on *her* own? What will her reaction be? I still haven't decided when I arrive home.

Chapter 13

As soon as I open the front door I hear the sound of my mother's voice and a man's I don't recognise. I enter the family room, noticing straight away the remains of an apple pie she must have made earlier and the empty cups and saucers, not the usual everyday mugs the two of us use. This is obviously a social occasion.

The middle-aged man wearing a smart suit I have found her in conversation with is obviously not here to sell life insurance or encyclopaedias. They stand up, and I think my mother looks rather uneasy as she says, 'Emily, this is Mr Booth.'

The man moves towards me and shakes my hand.

'I'm pleased to finally meet you Emily. I've heard so much about you from your mother.'

'Have you now?' I nod and smile, then furrow my brow with a look at my mother that says, 'what's going on?'. She ignores it and asks how my day has been.

I have no intention of discussing my day in front of a stranger, especially this day, so I say, 'Fine. How was yours?'

Mr Booth smiles; he's picked up this little mother and daughter by-play.

'I see your mother hasn't mentioned me. Please allow me to explain,' he says. 'I work in the Labour Exchange, as the Area Careers Officer. Your mother and I first met when she came seeking advice on how to become a librarian. That was several months ago, and I hope I'm not being too presumptive by saying that we've since become friends.'

My mother blushes, as she adds, 'I'm sorry, Emily. It was really up to me to tell you.'

I have to agree, but after taking in Mr Booth's smart clothes, confident manner, and educated speech, I compare him to my father, before replying.

'Yes, Mother, it was, but I'll forgive you if you tell me you've invited this nice gentleman to stay for dinner, so he can tell me what he thinks about my becoming a librarian.'

'Yes I have,' she says. 'And I've made a meat and potato pie.' She smiles, knowing it's one of my favourite dishes.

We have a nice meal, and although we talk a lot, I don't get to know a great deal more about being a librarian but I do find out that Mr Booth has a keen sense of humour and appears to have a genuine interest in my mother. After he has gone and we have washed up the dishes I get the whole story.

'I'm pleased you got on so well with him, and he seemed to like you. We've only met a few times. He invited me for a cup of tea at a café on the pretext of having more information about librarians, and since then we've met for walks.

'He's forty years old and has never been married, although he said he was engaged when the war started but while he was away his fiancée married someone else.

'He lives with his elderly mother in a house she owns in Elizabeth Street. I like him very much. He's easy to talk to and reminds me of Uncle Bob.

'I decided to invite him home to meet you and to see if you approved and to let him see just how poor I was before our relationship progressed any further.'

'You *are* a dark horse, aren't you? Keeping secrets from me, then surprising me like this. But he does seem nice, and I'm pleased you've met someone. I'm sure he's mature enough not to be concerned about how poor we are, and I'm sure he's impressed by your cooking and how clean you keep the house.'

I feel less like I am abandoning my mother now that she has someone else in her life. It's time to tell her my news.

She looks at me, as if seeing me for the first time. I don't mind such scrutiny, as I am proud of how I look. At seventeen, I'm five foot eight. There is no height on my mother's side, so it must come from my father. Fortunately, that's all I seem to have inherited from the Wilsons, as I have my mother's slim frame. My hair is fair. My nose? I consider it perfect, and I have a full mouth. My Aunt Jane once told me that I have an attractive face that shows too much character to be called pretty. She also keeps telling me that I am sometimes too smart for my own good.

My wide hazel eyes stare back at Mother and she blinks. This lets me know that although she was staring at me, she was not seeing me. She has apparently returned from wherever her mind had wandered as she smiles and takes hold of my hand.

After nodding to herself she says, 'I knew you'd have to move away to study, so I've been preparing myself for it.

'What you've said sounds all right, and I was younger than you when I first left home. Mind you, I wasn't living on my own. I had my big sister to keep an eye on me.

'I know you'll manage though, so give it a try. See how you feel in three months time. As it's Keswick, it's not too bad, being less than an hour away on the train if you get homesick.'

Chapter 14

I start work on the following Monday, and as Sarah is there during the first two weeks, Mr Peel is able to dedicate most of his time to me. I enjoy the work and apparently ask all the right questions, because he tells me he is pleased with my progress. He also makes time to give me a guided tour of the town and introduces me to some of the shopkeepers. This fits in well with my own plan, which is to use the weekends to explore the town and surrounding area instead of going home as my mother suggested.

However, I don't want Mother to feel neglected, so I get Mr Booth to arrange for her to be in his office each Friday, at one o'clock, so we can keep in touch by phone. This arrangement is also a means of allowing me to know that they are still seeing each other.

Three months go by and we agree on my staying a further six. I am enjoying the work and love the town. I feel sure that I can get used to this life.

At the end of the year I go home to spend Christmas with Mother and she tells me that Mr Booth's mother has passed away following a short illness, and that he has asked her to marry him.

They are married in January at the Registry Office. And, as Mother so elegantly puts it, I 'tart' her up for the occasion with a new dress and some skilfully applied makeup. I am her 'bridesmaid'. On account of her age and this being her second marriage, she's not doing the full bridal thing, so I don't have to wear a typical bridesmaid's dress, thank goodness.

Mr and Mrs Morgan and most of our family are there. Our family is made up of Uncle Arnold and Aunt Iris, my mother's younger brother Uncle Edgar, and Aunt Jane and Uncle Bob. My mother's parents, they are never called grandparents, are not included. They still live in Workington in the house that Mother and her siblings all grew up in but have still not spoken to my mother since her first wedding. My loyalty is to my mother, so I have made no effort to contact them.

I watch mother and Jane hold each other in a teary embrace just before the newlyweds leave for their honeymoon in Bowness.

'I think you've found your Bob,' I hear Jane say.

'Yes I think I have. I always knew I would one day,' Mother replies.

I move to Jane's side as we wave them off. She wipes a tear from her eye.

'This brings back some memories,' she says. 'We said goodbye like this in Oldham when I got married and went on my honeymoon. It was the first night in her life that we had not slept under the same roof. She told me how lucky I was to find someone like Bob and I told that her turn would come and there would be another Bob out there for her. I think she's finally found him. Your father's accident was the best thing that could have happened for her.'

'Yes, I agree,' I say.

**

After the honeymoon my mother and stepfather move into the house in Elizabeth Street that his mother has left him. The house is very nice. It's a terrace one, but it has three bedrooms and a large bathroom upstairs, two more rooms and a nice kitchen downstairs. And it has a rear exit. Perhaps more importantly, it's at the top end of town. Not much more than a mile in distance from Mother's previous home but a much greater distance in terms of the town's social structure.

Mother and I pay one last visit to the little house that holds so many bad memories for us and say goodbye to it. Once we move out it is never to be re-occupied, being declared unsuitable for human habitation. It's to be demolished.

With Mother happily settled, I am able to concentrate on my own future, and I decide to stay on in Keswick.

Chapter 15

By the time my twentieth birthday comes round I am a well-established member of the community. Keswick has truly become my home. Having exhausted all the exploring it is possible to do on my bike, I join a rambling club and see the area on foot. I am also a Friday night fixture in the bar of the Grey Mare, a popular hangout for the local young crowd.

My love life to this point has consisted of no more than a few evenings at the pictures with some of my fellow drinkers. I make it quite clear to them that I am not interested in forming an ongoing relationship. I have set my sights higher than a mere wage earner and I don't fancy a life as a farmer's wife. The rest of the Grey Mare's male patrons are already married.

My relationship with my boss has moved on from mutual respect, due to spending so much time together in the shop, to a genuine interest in each other's welfare. Although I am always careful regarding physical contact out of respect for his marital status, I can see no harm in a little mild flirtation to keep my hand in for when a suitable beau comes along.

I do, however, find myself occasionally fantasising about being a respectable married woman with a husband who owns his own business. I am not therefore, above giving John a hug and a peck on the cheek on his birthday, or at Christmas, and having noticed his lingering glances at my legs when my skirt rides up while I am on the ladder stretching to reach the top shelves, I am not above shortening my hems and stretching more often. God didn't give me these legs to keep them covered up, I decide. The cycling and walking have made them firm and they are as long and shapely as those of any chorus girl.

It is therefore with more than a passing interest that I begin to observe a gradual change in him. He has become less and less like the relaxed happy young man he was when I first started.

Business is good. I have been given several pay rises, so I don't think it is the shop that is bothering him. It has to be something in his private life and, although I am reluctant to risk upsetting our growing intimacy by probing too deeply into that, I want to know.

I have yet to meet John's wife, but her photo appears in the local paper almost every week. As the only child of wealthy parents and one of the town's more glamorous socialites, she is a member of every club and on every committee that is considered fashionable, but rarely is her husband photographed with her. The captions usually refer to her as Penelope, daughter of Ralph and Rhoda Thompson, rather than as Penelope Peel. I glean from local gossip that she and John were childhood sweethearts and had drifted into marriage without the full approval of her parents. They had hoped for a more prominent son-in-law than the owner of a bookshop. A professional man no doubt, a doctor or a lawyer perhaps. Those that have never seem to be satisfied with what they've got, I decide.

My first meeting with Penelope leads to my discovering the reason for John's unhappiness. I am on my own in the shop at the time. John has gone to the railway station to collect some parcels and there are no customers. I leave the shop unattended to bring some new acquisitions from the storeroom under the stairs, and although I am only gone a few minutes, I return to find an attractive, smartly dressed young woman using the ladder to access some of the higher shelves. I recognise some of the labels she is wearing and know that the nearest I can ever get to wearing any of them under my present circumstances is to look at them through a shop window. The expensive clothes and arrogant way she has availed herself of the ladder when there is a prominently placed sign that clearly states *Use of the ladder by customers is strictly prohibited, please ask for assistance* tells me that this just has to be Penelope Peel.

I say, 'Please come down and tell me what you're looking for, and I'll tell you if we have it.'

The woman turns and looks me up and down, with a look I would normally associate with that given to having found something unsavoury stuck to the bottom of my shoe. She speaks.

'As it is my husband' shop, and as there was no one in attendance, I decided to look for myself. I assume you are Miss Wilson.'

She turns her back to me and carries on looking through the books.

I have no intention of being so easily dismissed and say, 'Yes, my name is Emily Wilson, and I take it you are Mrs Peel. So, am I to assume you're aware that as you are not registered as being part owner, or listed as a member of the staff, that you are not covered by the accident insurance policy should you fall off the ladder and hurt yourself.'

This is the first retort that comes into my mind and although I say it with as much conviction as I can summon I have no idea if any of it is true. It has the desired effect, however. The older woman's back stiffens and she puts the book she is holding back on the shelf. She climbs very carefully down, before walking, without making eye contact, to pick up a pair of gloves she must have placed on the desktop and strides towards the door. She has apparently regained her composure by this time, as with the air of a woman who is used to having the last word she turns and walks back.

'Please let my husband know that I called in to remind him we are going to the Forsyths for dinner this evening,' she says, and opening her purse, takes out a sixpence and presses it into my palm. 'There's a good girl,' is her parting remark as she goes out the door.

Although I know it is childish, I make an exaggerated curtsy as the door closes behind her, and say, 'Oh! Thank you, thank you, m'lady.'

When John returns and I give him the message, he frowns.

'Don't you like the Forsyths?' I ask.

He looks at me for a few moments before replying.

'Jack Forsyth is Master of the Hunt this year and all night long they'll be talking about the next Meet and I'll be bored out of my mind.'

'But aren't you also a member of the hunt?'

'I was but I was always on the outer. I made too many remarks about hoping the fox would get away and got fed up of Penny saying that I hadn't a good seat. Penny's the energetic one in our family. Actually, we don't do a lot together these days. She's a keen cyclist and I'm not, and we used to be in your ramblers' club, but she wanted more strenuous walks and climbs than they undertook, so she recruited a few of her toffee-nosed friends and formed another club, with herself as president, so I dropped out.'

'That's disappointing, but haven't you known her since your schooldays. People do change as they grow older. You've a lovely home and a thriving business and she's very attractive and glamorous, so you must enjoy the physical side of your marriage. There's no need for you to do everything together to be happy.'

'A lovely home, eh? Daddy paid for the house we live in, and the furniture. All I have is this shop, which I love mind you, but they all want me to give it up and go into their family Real Estate business. If I do that, they'll own me completely. And yes, she is attractive and glamorous. Daddy gives her a generous allowance to buy all the clothes she wants.

'As for enjoying the physical side of our marriage, it's no better than the rest of it. We've been friends since childhood and as far as I knew, she'd had no other boyfriends, but she wasn't a virgin when we got married. In fact, she displayed far more sexual knowledge than I would have expected from a well brought up twenty-year-old woman. I was two years older than she was but had no sexual experience whatsoever. I felt like a sacrificial lamb on our wedding night. She took complete control. It was humiliating for me, to say the least. It didn't get much better either.

'She would never suggest sex after that, and whenever I did, she treated me in a condescending manner, as you would expect someone to treat a child who had asked you to play a game with them. She would smile at me, more of a smirk really. She would strip naked, then lie on the bed watching me get undressed, like a cat watching a mouse it was about to torment. And torment it was most of the time.

'She would make no effort to participate. She would lie there, with those big blue eyes wide open, watching me above her. I could never finish. Never reach a climax like that, with her watching me. Then she would smile that knowing smile of hers and roll me onto my back. She would lie by my side; her head propped up on one elbow and finish me off with her hand. All the time watching my face, knowing I was enjoying it, even though I didn't want to. Didn't want to give her that power over me. But I couldn't stop wanting her to do it.'

I notice that his stammer has come back, as it always does when he is nervous or excited. He has been talking as if I wasn't there and his candid and emotional confession has both moved and surprised me. It has taken our relationship to a new level of intimacy.

I decide that he must have wanted to unburden himself of his marital problems for a long time to be so frank. But what do I know about such things? The nearest I've got to having a physical relationship are the picture evenings with the locals or when I had half the sixth form fighting over who was going to take me up to supper at the annual school ball.

I am far too young and inexperienced to know how to answer, so I put my arms around him, to try and comfort him. We stand holding each other.

'Thank you for confiding in me. I had noticed you were a bit down in the dumps recently. Now I know why. I wish there was something I could do,' I say, hoping it is appropriate.

He looks at me for a long time before replying.

'You already do it. I've no right to say this, and I hope it doesn't affect our friendship, but I look forward to coming to work more than I do going away from it. You're the only one I enjoy talking to these days. I feel I'm closer to you than I am to Penny and I'm envious of all those young men who come in here to look at you while pretending to look at the books. I should have married someone like you.'

Wow! Where is this leading? I don't know but can't see any harm in encouraging him and I certainly don't want to discourage him. I take his hands in mine, and smile up at him.

'Nothing will spoil our friendship John, and you needn't feel envious of anyone. If you weren't in the shop every day, I would be a librarian by now. I'm pleased you've told me what it is that's making you so miserable. I don't know exactly how I can help you, but I am willing to try if you will let me. I'm sure everything will eventually turn out all right. My mother believes in fate and I'm beginning to agree with her. So, just you wait and see. Things are going to get better from now on.'

Something about what I have just said sounds familiar but the arrival of some customers curtails our conversation and I don't think any more about it. I truly believe what I have just told him. I am just not sure exactly how it is going to happen.

Chapter 16

Egg dumping is a popular old Cumberland tradition that takes place at Easter. And although it's two weeks after Easter the egg dumping competitions in the Grey Mare are alive and well. My friend Alicia and I are having a great time, even though my egg has made it through to the final and hers has been knocked out in the first round. We always share anything we win so she's as excited by my success as I am. I'm an experienced egg dumper; having fought several Easter campaigns, and have chosen well. My egg is only average size but it has a sharply pointed end that I have slyly polished with some lipstick, some spit and an old handkerchief, which is going to take a lot of washing before it comes clean. The eggshells have been dyed red so my secret weapon goes undetected.

There has been a lot of side betting up until now and a lot more is expected for the final. Several men have been to look at my egg to try and judge its chances before making their wager. Alicia and I have decided not to bet as we are guaranteed three pounds even if we only come second and a fiver if we win. There were thirty-two eggs at the start, each purchased for five shillings, making a total of eight pounds prize money. A consolation prize of this competition is that even if you lose you get to shell your egg and eat it.

The landlord announces that the final is about to begin and makes the draw.

'Number ten on top of number twenty-seven.'

Alicia gives a 'whoopee' and claps her hands. We have number twenty-seven and our preferred bottom hold.

Just as she says, 'I wonder who has ten?' I become conscious of a pair of male trousers appearing in front of me. I look up at their owner.

'I believe I am on top of you,' he says, with a broad smile on his face.

It is one of the other Friday night regulars at the Grey Mare, a young man from New Zealand, called Trevor Mitchell. He looks a few years older than me and has recently completed his university studies. He and three male friends are travelling the world before starting their working lives. They are popular with the patrons, challenging the men at darts and charming the girls. Trevor is captain of their rugby team and has organised the trip.

'Chance would be a fine thing, Trevor,' Alicia says, never short of a reply. 'Let's get the egg dumping out of the way first.'

Trevor's smile widens and my blush deepens. I recover quickly though and cup my egg in both hands leaving only the tip of the pointed end visible and the softer side shell inaccessible.

'You've played before,' he says. 'I can hardly see it.'

'Get on with it,' one of the onlookers says and Trevor gently taps my egg with his. No damage is done to either egg and he taps again. This time he stands up and examines his egg closely and then mine.

'Bugger! Mine's cracked,' he declares and offers his hand for me to shake.

'Number twenty-seven the winner,' someone calls out and the small crowd around us disperses, to collect or pay their wagers.

Trevor asks if he can join us, and Alicia, on her way to collect our winnings, winks at me behind his back.

She shortly rejoins us and we toast Trevor's cracked egg before he eats it.

Chapter 17

My friendship with Trevor has begun. He starts walking me home on Friday evenings and I feel attracted to him. He is tanned and handsome, stands six foot two and reminds me of Peter Finch. I've had a crush on Peter Finch since I saw him in 'A town like Alice.' But it is out of curiosity more than anything else, that I participate in, what Alicia calls 'shameful fumbling in the dark' with Trevor.

One Friday, after we have been celebrating one of his friends' birthdays and I have two glasses of champagne on top of my usual two beers, I invite him up to my room above the shop. We start kissing the moment we enter the room. I feel his tongue, smell his aftershave, *Eau Sauvage* by Christian Dior, the same as I bought John Peel for his birthday. I run my hands through his thick hair. Something I have wanted to do since I first saw him.

Oh God, don't let this be a mistake, I think, as he begins unbuttoning my blouse. Soon my skirt joins it on the floor and we fall onto the bed. I feel his hands on my breasts, my thighs, my buttocks and in a short while, although I can't remember him doing it, his shirt and trousers are off, and my hands seem to have a mind of their own as they move over his tanned, firm body. But it is purely physical. I feel curiously detached from what is happening.

Although I can feel his hands on me, I feel no emotion. Aren't I expected to cry out in ecstasy at this moment? My breathing is quite normal; there is no quickening of the pulse or shortening of the breath. Despite my inexperience of such matters I know enough about the male anatomy to feel he is aroused and begin some exploring of my own. I look down at the hand that has disappeared into his underpants, feel the silky, smooth, hard flesh beneath my fingers, and marvel at my boldness.

His hand slides down the front of my briefs and I feel his probing finger. He suddenly stops and sits up. He looks down at me and I realise he has discovered I am still intact.

'Surprise, surprise,' is all I can think of saying.

He tilts his head back and laughs,

'Surprise all right, there are no twenty-year-old virgins in New Zealand, at least not on the South Island.'

He is from Queenstown, which he has previously described as being the most beautiful place on earth.

Although we remain side by side and wearing only our underwear, I feel the flesh go soft in my hand.

'I'd better make us some coffee,' I say, and disregard my semi-nakedness to walk over to the sink.

Still in our underwear, we sip the coffee. The mood has gone.

'You are the first man I've allowed to take such liberties,' I confess, as if he wouldn't already have guessed.

He laughs again.

'More surprises, you even talk old fashioned. I'm flattered to be the first, but I would prefer not to have the deflowering of a virgin on my conscience when I'm only going to be around for a short time, thank you very much.'

It is then my turn to laugh, and I say, 'I admire you for being capable of such noble thoughts, Trevor. Would you like me to provide you with a list of the local girls I know who wouldn't trouble your conscience.'

We remain good friends after this and spend a lot of time together. Although it isn't easy, as he has found a job working in the hospital laundry to help pay for his holiday, and I have to share him with this, his mountain climbing and his three mates. Trevor continues to walk me home from the pub and we have the occasional evening at the pictures and he always kisses me goodnight but he never comes up to my room. This arrangement works well for me, as it is convenient to have someone considered as my boyfriend, in order to keep other would-be predators at bay while I ponder over my feelings for my boss and the situation regarding him and his wife, and what, if anything, I can do about it, or if I want to.

Although John hasn't mentioned Penny again since his outpouring, our relationship has become more intimate. The changes come slowly at first, just little things, like more touching. He leaves his hand on my arm or on my shoulder for just that little bit longer than is necessary. He smiles at me across the shop when it is full of browsers, and one day while I am on the ladder, he puts his hands on my hips, saying, 'Be careful up there.'

I like this new intimacy but I'm confused about my feelings for him. I want to let him know that I like it. I want to touch him back, but in the back of my mind I keep remembering that he is married. I want to know if he really has feelings for me, or if it's just my imagination. I even make sure he knows about my supposed boyfriend, to see if he will show signs of jealousy, or even interest, but he makes no comment.

We work later than usual one day, unpacking and cataloguing a large consignment of books, and it's after eight when we finish.

'That's a long job out of the way,' he says. 'You've really got the system going well. It would have taken twice the time before you came.'

'Thank you, but I get so absorbed in it that I hadn't noticed the time. You'll be late home.'

'No problem there. Penny is at one of her so-called meetings. Liaisons would be a better description, I think. I've heard rumours.'

'Things no better then?'

'Nor likely to be.'

I hesitate but only for a moment.

'Why don't you have a bite to eat with me then, as it's so late? I've some soup already made and some fresh rolls I bought this morning.'

His hesitation is less than mine, as if he's been waiting for the invitation.

'All right, I will. That would be nice.'

He switches off the shop lights and follows me up the stairs. It is dark as I open the door to my room and I am slow to find the light switch. He is close behind me and bumps into my back, his arms going around me for support, to prevent us stumbling. I start to laugh but he turns me around, still in the dark and his lips find mine. I am too surprised to immediately respond, so it is not a passionate kiss, more of a pressing together of our lips.

He draws away.

'I'm sorry, I shouldn't have taken advantage like that but I've wanted to kiss you for a long time.'

'It's all right,' I tell him.

I pull him back into me and we kiss again and then stand with our arms around each other in the dark. My fantasy springs to mind. This is the key to my dream of a respectable marriage and a successful business I am holding in my arms. I decide to be bold. It is now or never. This is as good a time as any to see if the key fits.

'Do you want to make love to me?' I ask.

'I do. I am in love with you and I hope my saying so doesn't spoil our friendship. I want to make love to you very much but not like this. You deserve better than a clandestine relationship. That would make me no better than Penny. My marriage is over, in all but name but I can't see any way out of it. Penny won't divorce me. Why should she? She does what she wants behind the curtain of respectability and her father would go out of his way to ruin me if I did anything to make out his precious daughter was anything less than perfect.'

I don't know what to say. Where does this leave me? The key is not yet available. I am more confused than ever.

'It's not a nice thing to say, but I've often wished her dead. Imagined her going out and not coming back. Having an accident or something. But it will never happen. I couldn't be that lucky,' he says.

I immediately think about my father's *accident*.

'Sometimes lady luck needs a helping hand.'

'What do you mean a helping hand? Like arranging an accident?'

'It wouldn't be the first one.'

'I could never do anything like that. Anyway the husband's always the first suspect if there are any doubts that it was an accident, that's if you believe the movies.'

'I was only joking. I know you could never do anything like that.'

'It's a thought though and it would leave me free.'

With that he kisses me again, more passionately this time and I feel his hands on my bottom, pulling me into him. Still in the dark, he leads me to the bed and we lie side by side, arms around each other. We don't speak for a while, each busy with our own thoughts. Mine wondering how far I am prepared to go to make my fantasy come true. I have gone the ultimate distance before to give myself the chance of a better future but this is hardly the same. It isn't a life-threatening situation. Or is it?

'I believe I could do it, if our roles were reversed,' I say, unconsciously putting my thoughts into words.

'Do what? You don't mean kill her.'

'Yes, if I thought there was no other way and my life was ruined as yours obviously is.'

'It certainly looks that way, but I can see no way out. You must be a much stronger person than I am. I've no choice. I'll just have to live with it and without you.'

Chapter 18

A whole month passes by, and I begin to notice a more morose John Peel with each passing day. He appears to have no interest in the shop and makes little or no conversation. The touching has also stopped, as if he has given up on forming any sort of relationship with me.

I, on the other hand, think about his predicament daily. I begin to imagine a life with him. Not so much the physical side of the relationship. I've already convinced myself after my 'shameful fumbling' with Trevor, that I will never experience the starry-eyed love of romantic novels. I compare the two of them. They are the direct opposite of each other. Trevor, all outdoors masculinity and a real man's man, as opposed to John, the mild scholarly loner. I don't really have the luxury of the choice to make but I know that what I really long for at this time in my life is the security and social status a marriage to a storeowner and respected member of the community will bring. My mind has stored a memory of the poverty and isolation that I endured in my early life and I can't erase it no matter how hard I try.

I enter the storeroom at the back of the shop and a startled John Peel turns away from me quickly, but not quick enough to avoid my seeing the tears in his eyes and the large handkerchief he is wiping them with.

'What is it John, what has happened?'

'I'm sorry you found me like this, I've been trying to hide my misery all week.'

'Tell me what has happened?' I insist.

'As usual, it's Penny. I had to make sure, you know, about the rumours, so I followed her last Sunday evening. She said she was going to her parent's house to discuss family business. That's why I wasn't invited. Not that I get invited much anymore, mind you. But this time for some unknown reason I was suspicious.

'She left the house on foot for a start, saying she fancied a walk. There was a car I didn't recognise in the next street, and as I came round the corner I saw her get in it. There was a man in the driver's seat. It was too dark for me to see his face but when she got in I saw them kissing.

'I'd been hoping the rumours were untrue, but now I know they're not. The whole town must be laughing at me or, worse still, feeling sorry for me.'

'Oh John, I'm so sorry. No wonder you're sad.'

'If only I weren't such a coward. I should leave her and to hell with the consequences. But I know that they'd try and ruin me and blacken my name, which would leave me with nothing to offer you.'

Although I'm upset at seeing him like this, I can only agree with him. I may not be able to have a fairytale romance, but I want security and social standing, not an ongoing feud with the Thompson family. I go to him and we embrace. The ringing of the shop doorbell interrupts the silence and I give him a squeeze and return to the shop. I have a feeling of desperation I haven't felt since just before the death of my father and see my hopes of a happy future fading away.

I realise I've been neglecting my friends at the Grey Mare recently and decide to catch up with them to take my mind off John and my immediate future.

It's only seven thirty when I enter and I notice it's busier than usual for this hour. The early Friday evening crowd is a motley bunch in summer, made up of hikers clad in sweaters, with cord trousers tucked inside their thick stockings, supping away at their pints of beer after a hard day on the fells. Shopkeepers and businessmen in suits sipping their scotch and sodas or gin and tonics, winding down after a busy week. And young smartly dressed people like myself just beginning an evening of socialising.

I spot Trevor leaning with his back to the bar in earnest conversation with a few of the regulars. I decide not to interrupt and go to the other end to buy my usual half pint.

'Busy early tonight,' I say to the barmaid.

'Been a busy week. I don't work Mondays as it is usually quiet but I was called in last Monday. Trevor's three mates were having a party to celebrate them leaving the next day for a sightseeing holiday in Europe. It's busy tonight because Trevor turned up with some friends. He's just announced that he's been offered a job back home and will be leaving in two weeks time,' she tells me.

This news makes me feel more miserable than ever, although I'm not sure why. I've ignored

Trevor for the past few weeks. I try to hide my sadness as I approach him to say goodbye. He seems unaware of it and gives me a big hug. Although Trevor is a serious mountain climber he has many friends among the ramblers and occasionally accompanies them on their walks.

'So, are you coming on my last hike?' He asks.

'Your last hike?' I echo, as Alicia joins us.

'Hi Em, haven't you heard? We're giving him a big send-off party here, a week on Sunday, but first we're all going on one last hike, in the afternoon. It'll be great. You should come along.'

They both look at me expectantly.

'Of course I'll come. Where are we going?

'Up Hindscarth,' Alicia replies.

Before I have time to comment, more people arrive and upon hearing the news begin to talk to Trevor. I take the opportunity to move across the room to view a map of the Lake District on one of the pub walls and find that Hindscarth, at 2385 feet, is one of the higher of The Derwent Fells. Far too serious for me, I decide, and wait for the opportunity to speak to Trevor.

'I'm not sure if I'm up to tackling a 2000 foot mountain,' I tell him.

'That's all right,' he says. 'It looks like I've been a bit ambitious in my choice of walks. There are now more ramblers than there are climbers going, so the ramblers have agreed to turn back at the Scope End Ridge, so you can join them, and we'll all meet up in the Grey Mare for the booze up later.'

**

On the day of the hike we all meet up in the Grey Mare car park. Not everyone has a car, so after deciding who is going in which car, proceed in convoy to Little Town. The weather is bright and sunny as we begin the walk. We head up the valley following the track that runs along the side of Newlands Beck before crossing the beck at the narrow footbridge near the long defunct Goldscope Mine.

The mine was once a rich source of copper and lead but is now only a reminder that picturesque Keswick was once the centre of smelting, with a dozen mines in the area. Having seen plenty of coal mine shafts near Workington I am surprised to see that the entrance to this mine is a hole in the side of a rocky slope. Although the track we are on is well marked and dry underfoot it is not an easy walk, as Scope End is 1348 feet high.

I manage to keep up with the leaders and look back to see the group is well spaced out. Trevor has been in the lead but he drops back to walk alongside of me. He gives me an encouraging smile and matches my pace towards the summit.

Not everyone bothers to climb the last few hundred yards or so to the very end of the Scope End ridge, as it twists around and rises steeply near the top. I find myself behind Trevor as we march in single-file with him in the lead. I decide it has been worth the effort as we stand side by side at the top. Looking back across Newlands Beck towards Derwentwater we can see Maiden Moor bathed in dappled sunlight, and the landscape in between is dotted with purples, pinks and greens from the still blooming heather and bracken. In the other direction, Robinson's lofty peak doesn't look quite as formidable with only a light mist shrouding its summit.

'You're lucky you've come on such a dry and clear day as there are a few stretches of bare rock that can be very treacherous in the wet and there's usually a lot of mist around this high up. I've been up here several times this summer. We would normally carry on up the ridge to Hindscarth and along to Robinson but you're walking in the mist most of the time, so this is the best vantage point,' Trevor says.

The others move back down the path but he holds my arm, slowing us down until we follow well behind.

'There's something I want to show you,' he says.

We walk on a few yards until we draw alongside a small shrub, apparently growing out of the fell side. He takes my arm again and surprises me by guiding me gently into a hollow concealed by the shrub. It is not big enough to be called a cave, but big enough to hold two people.

'This is probably the last chance we'll get to be alone, Em. So I'll say goodbye properly.' Trevor says, and before I can reply, he pulls me to him and kisses me.

It starts off as a gentle kiss; then, as I recover from the surprise and respond, he holds me tighter and kisses me firmly. Not now, Trevor, I think. I am having enough emotional traumas with John without you complicating things. We draw apart, and I look over his shoulder to see if we are being observed, giving myself time to recover my composure.

'Don't worry, no one can see us. The path twists round from here down. I'll miss you Emily,' he says, and I can tell he means it.

I stare up at him but can think of no words that will express the strange emotion that I am experiencing, so I squeeze him instead.

'We'd better join the others,' I say, knowing it is insufficient and the look on his face shows me that he too has been expecting more.

Chapter 19

Winter arrives early and a blanket of snow covers the whole of the Lake District by early December. Just what I don't need, confined inside the shop each day with few customers braving the cold to buy books and only John for company. His demeanour can best be described as moody, sullen, and occasionally, bad tempered. One day after he snaps at me for simply reminding him that he has a dental appointment, I can stand it no longer and, despite there being snow on the ground; I tell him I'm going for a ride on my bike. It doesn't take long for me to regret my hasty decision. It's all right on the busier roads because the snow ploughs have been out and sand spread on the surface to keep the traffic flowing, but once off them it is icy and treacherous. I almost turn back but the weather improves slightly, so, after letting some air out of my tyres to give me more grip, a tip given to me by Uncle Arnold, and finding this works, I keep on going.

 A short time later I'm glad I have, because although there are only shapes and not colours visible this day, the blanket of pristine snow that covers the landscape makes it a delightful sight. I pass an old farmhouse, the path by it barely discernible, so I make slow progress. I am beginning to enjoy the solitude but the further I go the more hazardous the terrain becomes. I decide to turn back before I reach the narrow bridge that crosses the stream. I have travelled this route many times and know that it is uphill on the other side.

As I am about to turn round I see another cyclist coming down the sloping path on the other side, towards the bridge.

As the cyclist draws nearer I can tell it's a woman, and watch in amazement as she accelerates down the slope. Then I realise she's not pedalling but braking hard, trying to slow her momentum.

The inevitable happens; her tyres lose their grip on the slippery surface and the bike slides sideways. The front wheel collides with the low wall that runs the length of the bridge on both sides, throwing her over the handlebars. Her head appears to hit the top of the wall before she disappears over it.

I lay my bike down and walk gingerly across the bridge. As I approach I can see gloved fingers on the wall. Looking over it I am astonished to see Penny Peel hanging by her fingertips, blood oozing from a cut on her forehead with her feet only inches above the frozen stream. The stream isn't wide but I know it to be deep in places. Penny looks up, her eyes wide with fear but not recognition. A scarf around my head as well as a cap conceals my face and as far as I know Penny has only seen me that one time in the shop.

'Help me,' Penny cries, her fingers flexing as they tighten their grip on the wall. She is trying to edge her way along the bridge towards the safety of the bank. Normally quick to react under any circumstances, I realise I am holding my breath.

I feel numb with shock, at first with the speed at which this has all happened and then at finding that the other cyclist is Penny. I simply look on.

John's words come flooding back to me. 'I have often wished her dead. Imagined her going out and not coming back. Having an accident or something.'

Is my mother right? Does fate determine our future? Despite the cold, my palms beneath my gloves are clammy with sweat. I feel both a part of and apart from the drama that is unfolding. I look around. There is no one else in sight.

One of Penny's hands disappears from the wall and she dangles there, defying gravity as she swings by one arm. She loses her grip and drops onto the frozen stream. She lands upright, then her feet slip and she falls backwards and lies spread-eagled on the ice. It appears at first that the ice is thick enough to support her, but as she struggles to get up, her feet sliding about, it begins to crack, with the cracks forming a spider web pattern around her. I finally snap out of my trance-like state and exhale loudly, feeling the tension drain out of me. It is too late. We lock eyes for a brief second, then, with a last despairing look Penny disappears through a large hole into the icy water.

The current here directs the water away from the bridge towards the point where the stream enters the adjacent river, so she is dragged under the ice. I wait a few anxious minutes to see if she will manage to break her way through. She doesn't reappear.

I return to my bike, sliding about on the slippery surface and peddle to the farmhouse. I notice smoke coming from the chimney, so I hope someone is inside. Knocking loudly on the door, I yell, 'Help, help! Someone please help! A woman's fallen in the stream and is under the ice.'

A middle-aged man opens the door and tells me to calm down. Between genuine sobs I tell him what has happened. He puts on a coat and a large pair of Wellington boots and follows me back to the bridge. He walks up and down the bank of the stream but keeps looking back at me and shaking his head.

'I'd better phone the police. You stay here in case she surfaces,' he says.

A cold wind has now sprung up adding to the chill of the day but I am oblivious to it. My mind races through the actual events as well as what could and probably should have happened had I remained my usual calm self. Could I have saved her? Or the horrible unthinkable alternative, which I didn't really want to contemplate? Would I have saved her?

I make a few important decisions.

Twenty minutes later two police constables arrive. They are well prepared wearing fishermen's waders and with one carrying a large axe and the other some blankets. They take one look at me before wrapping me in one of the blankets. They walk the bank, occasionally pointing at the ice before stopping at the place where the stream narrows and begins to bend towards the river. The one with the axe begins to smash the surface. The ice is apparently quite thin there as it breaks in large chunks revealing the dark water beneath. The other one steps into the water, bends low and peers under the ice looking back towards the bridge. He says something to his colleague who nods before he too enters the stream and begins another assault on the ice. They eventually reach down and rake around with the axe for a few minutes before standing up holding a body.

Laying the body on the bank they prod and poke it for a short while before covering it with the remaining blanket and carrying it back to the bridge.

'I'm afraid she's dead,' one of them tells us. He looks at the man from the farmhouse. 'I will go back to the station and report to my sergeant. He will want to talk to you both, so I suggest you stay in the house to keep warm until then.'

It's almost an hour later before a uniformed sergeant comes to the house.

'I'm Sergeant Outhwaite,' he announces. 'This must be very distressing for you, so I won't keep you long. We have identified the young woman. Her name is Penelope Peel.'

'Oh no!' I gasp. 'I work for her husband John.'

The sergeant exchanges glances with the farmer. 'My constables never said anything about you recognising her,' he says.

'I didn't recognise her. I was quite a way off when I first saw her coming down the hill. She was under the water by the time I got to the bridge. Then I came to the farmhouse to raise the alarm.'

'Close enough to tell it was a woman though,' he says.

'Yes, I could tell it was a woman.'

'Let me get this perfectly clear. You were coming from one side of the bridge and she was coming from the other, just like that? It's a strange day to be out cycling. Did you know she was out cycling? I mean did you arrange to meet her?'

'No, of course not. I work for her husband but I have only met her once. We have no social contact.'

'What a coincidence.' he says. 'All right that will be all for now. I'll just get your name and address and you can go.'

'My name is Emily Wilson and I live above Mr Peel's shop; The Old Bookshop.'

Sergeant Outhwaite writes this down, closes his notebook and then nods to himself as if for emphasis.

'Emily Wilson, yes of course. Now I remember, we've met before. I was a constable at the time but I came to your house in Workington, the night your father had his accident.'

'I recall a policeman being there,' I say, 'but I wasn't paying much attention, so I wouldn't have recognised you. Fancy you remembering my father's accident after all these years.'

'I remember it well. We had some concern at the time as to why he would climb the stairs in the dark when he could have switched the light on.'

I make no comment.

'I didn't expect you to remember me, but I told your mother that I thought you were taking it well and I remember telling you that you were a brave little girl. Sorry we had to meet again in such tragic circumstances.'

**

I am required to attend the coroner's inquest and tell the same story I told Sergeant Outhwaite. The deceased and I had approached the bridge from opposite directions. I was near enough to tell it was a woman but not near enough to recognise her. She had fallen off her bicycle and was over the bridge and under the water before I got there.

There are several references to the remarkable coincidence of my working for the deceased woman's husband and the coroner gets a scowl from the Thompsons when he says that the foolishness of cycling in such extreme conditions had contributed to the tragedy. A verdict of accidental death is recorded.

Chapter 20

John has never asked me directly if I had any part in Penny's death. This alone makes me suspicious that he thinks I had, considering how we'd talked about wishing her dead. I decide to let him wonder. The more he thinks I have helped him become a free man the better. I am also having my own crisis of conscience regarding the reason for my inaction at the scene.

Our relationship is progressing very slowly since the funeral. John is keeping up the charade of the grieving husband, although I can see a renewed zest for living in him whenever he is away from public scrutiny. Penny's parents have been less discreet in hiding their true feelings. They no longer pretend to like their son-in-law and have taken back the car, which they had paid for and was registered in Penny's name, and give him little notice when they decide to sell the house they own, which John and Penny had been living in. He receives nothing from the sale and comes out of his marriage of seven years with no more than he had when it started. Probably less, as with me living in the room above the shop he has to pay for accommodation in a guesthouse. But the bookshop is doing well and he can afford it.

Almost a year passes before we start officially dating. Although we have on occasions been seen lunching together in public while he was married, as colleagues might, it causes a few tongues to wag when he starts going out to dinner with his attractive young shop assistant once he is widowed, even after a lapse of twelve months. We have agreed on discretion in public.

John is very careful to be back in his lodgings at a reasonable hour each evening, so as not to give his landlady cause to add to any gossip that might be going around. Not that there has been anything to gossip about at this stage. The nearest we have got to any form of physical relationship is a few kisses when we say goodnight. Not that that bothers me. It's not the physical side of a marriage I'm interested in. However, I'm becoming impatient and decide he must be feeling insecure, that he's afraid of being made to feel inadequate again if he starts another physical relationship. Afraid he might be hurt again. I decide it is time to take the initiative.

One Saturday evening we return to the shop following dinner at the Lodore Swiss Hotel, and I can tell by his fidgeting that he's hesitant about getting out of the car. Business at the bookshop has been good enough to allow him to buy a two-year-old Hillman Minx, which makes it easier and quicker to travel around the countryside to search the auctions and deceased estates for valuable and rare old books. It has also improved our social life. I take hold of his hand.

'It's early yet, John. Come inside for a while,' I say, getting out of the car quickly so as not to give him the chance to refuse.

I unlock the front door, but don't put on any lights until I reach the stairs. He follows me up.

I turn and put my arms around his neck and kiss him on the lips.

'Thanks for a lovely evening, the dinner was delicious.'

He smiles and puts his arms around my waist.

'I don't want to spoil the lovely evening, John, but it's been over a year since Penny died, and I remember you saying you wanted to make love to me very much. Now you can but you haven't. And what about you being in love with me? That implied marriage to me. I think almost eighteen months is long enough to play the grieving husband. Especially as you said everyone knew Penny was playing fancy free and making a fool of you. Why are you so concerned about our relationship becoming public knowledge?'

He stands silent for a while, and I begin to think I have upset him, but he surprises me.

'You are right; I have been slow to take it all in. You know what I mean, being free of Penny, being able to start again. Why don't we go away for the weekend? We can close the shop on Saturday; it's going to be fine again. Let's go to Blackpool where we can get lost among the crowds. We can be Mr and Mrs Smith for the weekend.'

That's a start, I decide.

'Yes, let's do that. But why don't we avoid the crowds and go to Morecambe instead. It's just as nice and it's nearer. And we wouldn't need book in advance. It will be easy to find a room there in one of the hotels away from the main front,' I say.

It's an exceptionally warm autumn night so we leave the windows and curtains open when we retire to our bedroom. I throw back the covers on my side. I am wearing a carefully selected flimsy nightgown and although it is not transparent, I know that when I walk to the open window and stand looking out at the moonlit sea, to supposedly cool off, the bright moonlight will make it appear so.

It works. 'You look beautiful Emily, come back to bed,' he says.

I do and we embrace and begin kissing passionately. Again I feel a man's hands exploring my body and again feel no emotion. Although we are doing this for his benefit rather than mine, I do begin to wonder if there is something not quite right with me. Perhaps I am emotionally scarred through my life with my repressed mother. I always need to be in control. Have I lost the ability to trust?

I have deliberately not discussed the physical side of our weekend away with him, not being sure if sex was on his agenda and not wanting to put any pressure on his already weakened self-confidence, so I have not thought about birth control precautions. Now it is too late, but I decide that if I do get pregnant, all well and good.

I can feel him hard against me but remembering what he told me about Penny humiliating him on their honeymoon, I feign complete ignorance. I am reluctant to spoil the moment but wanting to boost his libido by showing that I expect him to be like any other normal male in this situation and want to have sex and ever the practical one and still very much in control, I bid him stop.

'Wait John, just one moment.'

I walk to the chest of drawers and return with a large bath towel. There is still enough moonlight to see his smile as I lay the towel down on top of the sheet and myself on the towel. He removes his pyjamas and then my nightgown and we begin again, this time with more urgency. I again feel his hardness again against my leg as he moves over me. I stretch my arms upwards around his neck in what I hope he will take as a gesture of complete surrender. I begin kissing his chest, my eyes closed. His finger probes and finds an obstruction. He lowers himself and penetrates me in a series of gentle but firm thrusts. It is all over quickly after that and he moves off me. He wraps his arms around me.

'Are you all right? Did it hurt?' He whispers.

'I'm fine, and no it didn't hurt. Was I all right for you?'

'You were wonderful, I feel as if I've just done it for the first time too.'

A short while later, wearing our robes, we quietly, it is almost midnight, make our way to the bathroom at the end of the hall. John runs a warm bath and I lie in it while he sits on the edge and sponges me down. It has not hurt and there is very little blood on the towel.

There are several more weekends away. And we make love frequently in the room above the shop. A few months later he proposes and we agree to get married before the end of the year.

Chapter 21

As John's previous wedding was an elaborate one, as befitting the daughter of one of the town's leading families, and as we have no friends to invite, Alicia my only remaining friend from the Grey Mare days being away at university, we decide to make our wedding a quiet one and away from Keswick. We are married at the Cockermouth Registry Office. My mother wants me to wear a white bridal gown, but I don't think of myself as a blushing bride and the practical side of me wins out. I convince her to settle for me wearing a smart off-white suit, with a wedding veil as a compromise. John's parents both died young, so the guests consist of my mother and stepfather, whom I now call Peter; Jane and Bob; and Iris and Arnold. Iris's oldest daughter Margaret is my only bridesmaid.

I am as pleased about the wedding for my mother's sake as for mine. Her own marriage continues to prosper, and John and I visit them regularly. She and her brother Arnold have a strained relationship since her wedding, which I put down to jealousy. Her social status has improved with her respectable marriage and her move to Elizabeth Street. She has given up her job, but as she now lives close to Portland Square, she keeps up her friendship with Mrs Morgan and they occasionally have lunch together.

Peter has bought a car and they have begun having frequent holidays around the country. Arnold and Iris on the other hand now have three children, which keeps them poor. Also, mother never visits the bottom end of town where Arnold lives, a gesture designed to help erase the painful memories of her past.

My wedding bridges the gap and I am pleased to see them all together again, chatting away about childhood memories. Arnold tells us that he rarely hears from Edgar, who is now living in Glasgow. He has married a local girl and invited none of his family to the wedding.

For two years after our wedding we live in the room above the shop and as far as I am concerned it is satisfactory. I have achieved my objective. I have my respectable businessman and his business. However, I begin to notice a change in John. He appears to be going out of his way to renew his friendship with some of the more prominent members of the community, people who have avoided him since his previous in-laws excluded him from their elite social circle.

I begin to wonder if he is missing the instant respect that being a member of the Thompson family offers, despite the terrible price he was paying for it. Whenever we are invited to dinner parties and other social engagements, I play the dutiful wife but only feel accepted when they are business-related occasions. I feel I have earned the respect of the businessmen of the town but can't muster up any enthusiasm for small talk with their wives. I am also younger than most of the other women so they eye me with more than a little suspicion whenever I am seen in deep conversation with their husbands.

Our business is doing well, we are making plenty of money, and John suggests that perhaps it is time we consider starting a family. I can think of no reason not too; having achieved the security I want but still feel there is something missing in my life. Perhaps it *is* a family of my own. Up until now I have used sex as a way of helping John regain his confidence and his dignity and binding him to me, controlling him. However, he makes love like he does everything else, methodically and efficiently, and, I'm sure my friend Alicia would add, boringly. I listened carefully to what he told me about his life with Penny and although I didn't gain any personal pleasure from the act, I quickly mastered the art of pretending I did. Having read *The Kinsey Report* and other sex manuals, I consider myself theoretically prepared for the task and being aware of what he didn't like about his previous sex life, I know what to avoid. Now with my mission accomplished and John convinced it had been Penny's fault for his lack of sexual prowess, we have settled down to what Alicia calls, 'the married woman's once a week if you are lucky' routine. We have not previously discussed having a family and I have been using a diaphragm up to now, so I have not yet tested my ability to conceive. It was not a problem for my mother, yet her sister could not; 'the Lord works in mysterious ways his wonders to perform', as they might say in the Salvation Army. I decide to stop using the diaphragm and let fate, in the guise of nature, take its course.

'All right, I agree, let's try,' I say to John, in the shop a few days after he made the suggestion.

He looks surprised for a moment. 'Ah! Try for a baby you mean. Good.'

'There's just one thing though, the room upstairs is hardly perfect for child rearing. Supposing we're lucky right away. Perhaps we should look for a small house.'

'Thought you might say that,' he replies, and goes behind the counter to pick up the phone. He stands with his back to me and speaks quietly so I'm unable to hear what he says. He puts the phone down.

'We're going to meet Horace Needham at two o'clock, to look at a house.'

'That was quick. Any particular house?' I ask.

He looks sheepishly at me. 'I've been looking around for some time and there is one I think would be perfect. It's only a few streets away from here.'

I don't like decisions made for me, especially when they are made furtively. I also know that houses around this area are very expensive. Some of these thoughts must have shown on my face.

'Don't say anything until you've seen it please,' he says.

So I don't.

We shut the shop just before two and begin walking towards the town centre, turning right down a short narrow street and doubling back slightly down another one. I can see Horace Needham's short plump figure standing outside what looks like a row of Victorian town houses.

He has long curly hair, and dresses in an old fashioned manner, looking as if he has just stepped out of a Dickens' novel. But he is the only Real Estate Agent in town who has managed to thwart Penny's father from having a complete monopoly of the local housing market.

'Good afternoon, John. Good afternoon, Emily. Lucky you phoned when you did. I have someone else very interested in this property,' he greets us.

Fancy trying that one on us, I think. We say that all the time about rare books; the more expensive the item, the more people who are supposedly interested. There is one minor blemish on the viewing prospectus; however, after I read the sign in the window of number Eleven Crosthwaite Place and see the asking price. Can we afford that much?

'Let's go inside shall we,' Needham says.

We follow him in. It is indeed a two-storey Victorian Terrace house, as described on the notice, one of the middle ones in a row of four, and well preserved. I love it straight away. There is a hallway, an open plan living/dining room, a nice kitchen, plus two bedrooms, on the first floor, and two bedrooms and a bathroom on the second. The kitchen and bathroom have been modernised but tastefully, so as not to detract from the overall ambience. It has little bay windows at the front. I even liked the name, *Oak Cottage*.

I am left to wander around on my own as the men discuss the important matters, such as price, and rates, and what a grand investment it will make, as well as being a lovely home for a nice young couple. We leave with the promise to give it our full consideration and make a decision in the morning.

We are silent until we reach the shop. Then John says, 'What did you think? You took your time looking around. I bet you like it.'

'I do, but it's very expensive. I was thinking of something cheaper and more modern, with a garage. There's only street parking. They drove horses in Victorian times.'

'Modern, you mean on the outskirts of town. Waste of money. These Victorian houses are like rare books. They grow in price. Think of how much it will be worth in, say, five years from now. It will be an investment, as well as a nice home to live in. The shop is doing well. We can afford it. We could have it furnished and be settled in before the baby came. And it's so close to the shop and the town. Mr and Mrs Peel, of *Oak Cottage*, it has a nice ring to it.'

Why don't I let my heart rule my head for once? A few years ago I would have scoffed at the suggestion that I would ever own a house like this one, and here one is, within my grasp. So why do I hesitate? I have lived in poverty all my life, moving from the old house into a one room flat wasn't all that much of an improvement.

I have worked and schemed hard to get where I am today. Could this be the final step I have to take to escape the poverty cycle forever?

John is right. We probably can afford it and we already have enough saved for the down payment. I begin to imagine the house filled with antique furniture and the look on my mother's face when I show it to her. Mother and Peter could stay overnight when they visit, instead of driving home after dinner. Aunt Jane and Uncle Bob could come for holidays. For the first time in my life I begin to feel like a woman of substance. I know I can get to like this life.

'You're right, I like it,' I say. 'In fact I love it and I agree it's a good investment. I'm still nervous about spending so much money though. Why don't you go and talk it over with old Simpson at the bank, to see what he thinks? You would have to borrow the money from him anyway, wouldn't you?'

He smiles, and surprises me again.

'I already have. It seems Needham *has* had a few people interested, and one of them had enquired about a loan from our bank, so Simpson already knew about the property. He also told me in confidence how much I should pay for it. Seems Needham has been told by the owners to reduce the price to sell it. And because I own the shop, you know, not lease it like most of the shops in town, and because we bank with him and he knows how well the business is doing, he said he would lend us the money. Plus enough to buy furniture with, so we could buy it all at once.'

I am pleased to hear what he's just said, but not pleased to hear that it's all gone on behind my back. Perhaps I'm not as much in control of him as I think.

'You appear to have it all worked out. Why bother about my opinion?' I say, pouting my lips.

'Don't be upset. I wanted to surprise you. I knew you'd like the house. And besides, you deserve it. The shop's success is mostly your doing. You have everything so well organised, you know the businesses as well as I do now.'

He's right. I do like the work and I won't have to give it up if we have a child. We can turn the room upstairs into a nursery and I can spend most of my time in the shop. I want to let him see I'm still annoyed though.

'I suppose you'll now confess that you've borrowed the money and bought the house.'

'No, I didn't go that far. But if you agree, I'll go to see Needham and make him an offer based on the price old Simpson mentioned,' he says, looking pleadingly at me.

'Mr and Mrs Peel, of *Oak Cottage*. It does have a nice ring to it,' I say, 'but promise not to go and make any more big decisions behind my back.' He comes over and hugs me.

'Mind the shop; I'll go to see Needham right away.'

We move into the house six weeks later and our first dinner party is to celebrate my mother's fiftieth birthday. She's very impressed even though it's only partly furnished. We did borrow enough to buy the furniture all at once but have promised ourselves we'll be selective in choosing the right pieces.

'I like your new home *and* your husband. You've done well for yourself,' Mother tells me in a quiet moment.

'So have you, Mother. I told you that things were going to get better for us. People get what they deserve in this world.'

Nineteen fifty-eight is a good year for us, but nineteen fifty-nine is even better. Following the introduction of commercial television broadcasting in nineteen fifty-five, there was a slump in book sales for a few years while the country got used to this new phenomenon but since the novelty wore off, the demand for books has been greater than before.

The Macmillan-led Conservatives took over the running of the country and Macmillan's battle cry, 'You've never had it so good,' has been true for most of the population. Commercial television brings nightly demonstrations of the latest consumer products into everyone's home, making the term 'working class' almost obsolete. Most households now boast a refrigerator and a washing machine. And a third of the population own a car.

Any doubts I may have been harbouring about our ability to afford the house are now gone. We don't allow the spending frenzy to pass us by either and though we've so far stuck to our plan to buy furniture befitting the architecture, we furnish one of the downstairs bedrooms with modern furniture and modern appliances, a television and a radiogram.

John is travelling further afield now in search of rare and antique books and occasionally stays overnight, to spend a day or two scouring the small villages in the northeast, or in Lancashire or Yorkshire. I try to manage on my own for a while when he is away but eventually we decide to employ Sarah, his former assistant, for a few hours each day. She knows the job, the money is a help to her and Sarah's mother is able to look after her baby.

Our increasing affluence allows me to learn to drive and have a car of my own. I don't know anything about cars but fall in love with one particular car. The salesman says it is a 1955 Morris Minor Traveller, Series Three as if trying to impress me with its name and pedigree. John tries to put me off it by saying it only has two side doors, but I now have an optimistic approach to life and am in a buoyant mood. So, although I have noticed it has the practical advantage of wide opening back doors that will help when I'm loading my bike or hiking equipment, I choose it simply because I like the look of its wood framed rear.

Chapter 22

Although it's still summer, which in Keswick means hordes of visitors, fell-walkers, mountain climbers and general sightseers, I've managed to find a parking space on Main Street, close to the grocer's shop from where I have just emerged carrying a box of groceries. It's been packed for me from a list I left earlier today. As I bend to place the box into the rear of my car, I hear a voice behind me crying out, 'Mrs Peel, Mrs Peel.'

I turn and see Tommy the young man from the shop hurrying towards me, holding a parcel wrapped in white paper.

'I'm pleased I caught you before you drove off. This is your butter and cheese. I was serving someone else when you came in and Dick handed you the box. I packed it myself this morning but kept these in the cool room until you came to collect it. Dick didn't know it was there of course.'

He says it all in such a rush that he is almost out of breath. I notice his face is pink but don't think it's from exertion. Dick, the shop's owner has previously told me that Tommy has a crush on me.

I take the parcel from him.

'Thank you, Tom,' I say, remembering not to call him Tommy to his face as so many of the customers do. Most seventeen-year-old boys like to be treated as mature adults, especially by a twenty-six-year-old woman like me, who wears her hemlines as short as decency allows to show off her long slim legs and who likes to dress in the latest fashions.

I look over his shoulder as he turns to leave and notice some scaffolding has been erected outside a shop I know to be vacant. It was not there two days earlier when I last drove down Main Street, so I call after him.

'Do you know what's going on there, Tom?'

He turns and sees where I am pointing and is an even darker shade of pink when he answers.

'They've started painting the outside and fitting out the inside.'

'Yes I can see that, but what sort of business is it going to be?'

This time, red is nearer his colour.

'It's a bookstore Mrs Peel; Cartwrights'.'

This explains his deepening colour. No one likes to be the bearer of bad tidings, and telling someone who up until now has been running the only bookshop in town that a branch of the biggest bookstore chain in the north of England is about to open and on the town's busy main street at that were bad tidings indeed. I am too shocked to speak but manage a nod of acknowledgement in his direction allowing him to escape to the safety of the grocery store.

I drive home and am once more lucky, finding a parking space outside my front door. Although this is a residential area, it is only a few streets away from the centre of town and closer to the lake, so visitors often park here. I'd have walked to town if it had not been for the weight of the groceries. I unpack them and put them away and walk another few streets in the direction of the lake, to The Old Book Shop. There are no customers present and

John is unpacking a large cardboard box and stacking its contents on the shelves.

'Did you know that Cartwrights' were opening a branch on Main Street?' I ask him, without preamble.

He continues with the unpacking for a few moments, then replies. 'Yes and no. I heard they might be sometime last year. Are you now telling me that they are?'

He seems to be taking the news more calmly than I am.

'You didn't mention it.'

'It might never have happened and there was nothing we could do about it anyhow. Also, there are two butcher's shops and two grocery stores in the town and they still manage to prosper. How did you find out?'

'Tommy told me. They are fitting Postlethwaites' old shop out. Meat and groceries are hardly the same as books though, are they? Everyone has to eat but not everyone buys books and we won't be able to compete in the new book market with the buying power of a chain store.'

'We'll just have to try harder with the old and rare books then, won't we?' He smiles at me as he says it.

'You're taking this very calmly. What's going on?'

'Nothing's going on. I just think it's too early to start worrying.'

I'm not convinced, but don't reply. I start straightening the books on the shelves. He obviously isn't in a communicative mood, so after gazing out of the window at the bright sunshine for a while, I feel the need to be on my own.

'It doesn't look as if I'll be required here on a day like this. I don't expect there'll be a rush to be indoors browsing through books. I'll go and get the dinner started.'

He nods his agreement, and I walk out of the shop.

Chapter 23

'Morning, Archie. Those pork chops look good. I'll have two and four pork sausages please,' I say to my favourite butcher.

'Good enough to eat they are, eh Sam?' he replies, winking at his young assistant. 'Are you going to the Playgoers on Friday, Emily? I've got some tickets for sale.'

'Sorry, Archie, I'm not really a fan of Oscar Wilde. Hope it's a success for you though,' I tell him, knowing he has a leading role in the local production of *The Importance of Being Earnest*.

Having now been married for five years and proving ourselves by running a successful business and buying an expensive house, we have been accepted into the local society. The decision to accept us was eased by the retirement of Penny's father and the Thompsons' subsequent move to live by the seaside, in Bournemouth.

John has been invited to join the Golf Club, although he is not much of a golfer, and with him playing on Sunday mornings I have regained my enthusiasm for rambling. There is only the one rambling club in town now that Penny's club has disbanded following her death. Although I still don't consider us as being part of the 'in crowd', we do get invited to most of the events on the Keswick social calendar.

I come out of the butcher's and walk across the road to Cartwrights'. They are having their first anniversary sale.

'Morning, Emily. Sell you anything?' the shop manager says, greeting me with a broad smile. We had an uneasy relationship when they first opened. He had been aware of the situation and hadn't expected to be welcomed warmly. We have since become friends after he'd walked into our shop carrying a bunch of flowers. He said they were a peace offering, adding that he only worked for the firm and went where they sent him.

As anticipated, our new book sales have dropped dramatically, but we have managed to sell a few of our more expensive old and rare books, which helped absorb the initial loss. However, the future looks bleak. We have had to stop employing Sarah, have cancelled all our orders of new books and are selling the current stock at half price.

'Morning, Geoffrey. No, you can't sell me anything, I'm just here to check out the layout so that I can find my way around when I come looking for a job as a sales assistant.'

Although I'm half joking, the idea of having to consider working for someone else has crossed my mind and I don't like it. When I arrive back at the shop, which I had closed for lunch, I find it already open and John inside.

'You're back early. I wasn't expecting you until tomorrow.'

'My luck was out this time. I arrived too late at most places and found that some of our rivals had beaten me to the punch. Anything worth having had already been taken,' he explains. 'But I did get an idea.'

'It'd better be a good one, as I've sold nothing in the last day and a half.'

'We could become a second-hand book exchange. They're springing up in all the larger towns, and with the volume that Cartwrights' are selling, there should be a lot of second-hand books around Keswick.'

'Second-hand books? That's hardly the same as old and rare is it? Have we fallen so low? What would your father say?'

'My father was a very practical man. He would agree with me. But don't think of it as us having fallen. We'd just be providing a different service to the community. And by making money out of the books that Cartwrights' are selling, we'd be getting our revenge.'

'Now I like the sound of that. OK, tell me how it works.'

The conversion to the second-hand book market is an instant success and with the help of some astute advertising our revenue returns to its previous high level. Sarah rejoins us, working more hours than before.

Chapter 24

With our financial problems out of the way I am able to turn my mind to other issues. I have still not fallen pregnant. My periods are as regular as clockwork. We have consulted our doctor, Dr Brennan, and had tests done, which show no physical reason for our failure. We have also gone from a 'married woman's once per week if you're lucky' situation, to a 'quick, John, my body temperature is just right' situation, with the only result being to put John off sex altogether, as he finds he can't perform on cue.

We agree to stop trying so hard and let nature take its course. That is until I come across another Dr Kinsey's report, this time a 1953 one entitled *Sexual Behaviour in the Human Female*, and begin to wonder if I'm missing out on something by allowing our copulating to be only a means of satisfying John and if possible produce a baby, without any thought to my own pleasure. I remember what he told me about feeling humiliated when Penny took control, so I know I have to be careful in my approach to anything new.

'I had another talk to Dr Brennan about our problem getting pregnant and she suggested that we should try a few different positions when we were having sex,' I casually mention to him one evening.

He doesn't show any interest.

Later that evening I delay my entry when we retire to the bedroom to allow him time to get into bed. He's reading when I arrive.

'What's that you are reading?' I ask, not really wanting to know.

'This month's *Country Life*,' he says and looks up as he says it.

My dress has been unbuttoned and as he looks up I let it fall to the floor. I stand there in my pants, bra, suspender belt and stockings.

'It came today,' he continues, still looking up.

I reach behind me and undo my bra. Holding it in one hand I do a few stretching exercises. 'You men are lucky you don't have to wear these things,' I say.

'Yes,' he agrees.

I slowly remove my stockings, imagining I can hear striptease music playing in the background.

'You mentioned Dr Brennan suggesting we try different positions to help you conceive.' He has heard after all and something must have just jogged his memory.

'Did I? Yes, I think I did,' I reply, toying with the elastic at the top of my briefs.

'What sort of positions, did she suggest?'

'Well, she didn't really make any specific suggestions. Probably the ones in the pictures in the booklets she gave me to read, when I first went to get the diaphragm fitted,' I tell him, giving him a full frontal while pretending to examine the briefs I am now holding.

'Can you remember them?'

'Yes, I think I can remember some of them. Do you want to try some, to see if it helps me to conceive?'

I sometimes surprise myself by my ability to carry out such scheming. He's more than a willing participant after that and I eventually get a turn on top.

Alicia has confessed to doing a lot of sexual experimenting while she was attending University and has described in vivid detail the various ways she has used to prolong her male partners' climax. I practice most of them on John and achieve orgasm after orgasm. He isn't aware of my academic assistance and simply thinks he's getting more experienced. After one particularly lengthy session, he tells me he now knows what it must have been like for Errol Flynn and that perhaps he should send a bouquet of flowers to Dr Brennan.

Despite our experimenting and increased activity, I do not fall pregnant. Our enthusiasm gradually declines. My flimsy nightwear is exchanged for neck to knee pyjamas, while reading a book before lights out is the only urge John seems to get.

Our marriage in general also declines, with neither one of us bothering to make the effort to do anything about it. I put this down to the fact that we are approaching our seventh year, and perhaps there really is a seven-year itch.

I realise John has changed more than I have. Almost overnight he's become more confident and I don't think it's all to do with his feeling like Errol Flynn. He begins to involve himself in local affairs. He joins the Rotary Club and the Conservative Club and gets himself elected to the local council. He stops going away as much and on a few occasions when we receive a tip-off that a particular auction may have some valuable books, he suggests that I go instead, citing his attendance being required at important meetings as the reason.

Although we are now spending a lot less time together, I don't object. It isn't as if I've married him for love or his sparkling conversation, and I have plenty to occupy my time. I'm virtually running the shop on my own, and I enjoy the business trips away as they give me the opportunity to scour the antique shops looking for any furniture bargains as well as books. I do think it ironic, however, that John is now mixing with the so-called elite people of Keswick, and the same sort of snobby people he has criticised his former wife Penny for associating with.

One notable point of discontent comes when he suggests doubling our mortgage repayments to the bank.

'While all is going well with the business, we should reduce our debts, in case we have another setback, like Cartwrights',' he tells me.

'Yes, John, I can see the sense in that, but we've been putting surplus money aside for such an eventuality and it gives me a lot of comfort to know we have some ready cash available. We won't be able to save as well as double the repayments.'

He hands me a sheet of paper. 'Look at this. It's a new evaluation of the house. Old Simpson gave it me. See how much the value had increased in the five years since we bought it.'

I read it carefully, noting Simpson's recommendation to increase our investment in our house.

'Didn't you promise not to do things behind my back?' I say.

'I haven't done anything yet. We're discussing it now,' he replies rather curtly.

'And why did he show you the valuation? Did you ask him for it?

'The matter of property prices came up at a meeting that Simpson, Needham and I attended. Needham began telling me what a bargain I'd got when I bought the house, and I asked Simpson to confirm it by giving me the bank's estimation of its value.'

'If you'd get into the habit of letting me know in advance what you're planning, it wouldn't appear so furtive,' I tell him in my best peevish tone.

'As you are aware by my frequent absences from the shop, I've had a lot of meetings lately. It just slipped my mind.'

It seems like a poor excuse, but I think I have made my point.

'All right then, arrange to increase the payments but only while we continue to do well, or a miracle happens and we have a baby.'

John has looked very tense during the conversation. He appears to relax a bit with my last remark but not completely. Later I begin to wonder if his relaxing is due to the prospect of having a child or at my agreeing to increase the repayments.

I'm more in control of the baby situation than he knows. He's not the only one who can be furtive. Having first thought that having a child would stamp the seal on what I consider a satisfactory marriage, financially anyway, I'm now less confident. I'm now dividing my opinion between a child bringing us closer together or increasing the widening gap that has appeared in our relationship.

I've therefore renewed my acquaintance with Dr Brennan and asked her to prescribe some birth control tablets. I have gone 'on the pill', as Alicia would have put it. They were first made available commercially in 1961 and Alicia had been one of the first to try them. As she's not fallen pregnant during the two years since with her promiscuous lifestyle, I've decided they must work.

Dr Brennan was disappointed when I first approached her, mainly at hearing our marriage was floundering and my asking her not to mention the pills to John. She suggested that I consider my decision very carefully before jumping onto the Women's Lib. bandwagon, and I assured her that I would.

Chapter 25

Although as usual I've been awake since six o'clock, I find myself dawdling. Perhaps this is what happens as you get older. My thirtieth birthday is only a month away. I notice John looking at his watch several times during the next thirty minutes. It's been a while since we've both gone to the shop at the same time on the same day and although we're both going there today, he'll shortly be leaving again to a pre-auction deceased estate sale in Grasmere.

'All right, I'm ready. Let's go,' I say, and follow him out of the door. I turn round to lock it when a car pulls up, then stops and double-parks next to my car. I finish locking the door and turn to see Horace Needham beckoning to John from the car's open window. I go to join them, but having spoken a few quick words to John as he bends towards him, Horace Needham drives off without a glance in my direction.

'Good morning to you too, Horace,' I say. 'What was all that about?'

'Err, some urgent council business. Sorry, Emily, but I might be tied up all day.'

'What about Grasmere?'

'I don't know what there'll be there. The information I got was very vague, but as it was Grasmere, well, I thought it was worth a look. Would you mind asking Sarah to come in today and going yourself?'

He looks worried, which makes me worried. I am also annoyed. He's spending more time on so-called council business than he is at the shop these days. Or perhaps it's because I don't like any of his council colleagues, especially Simpson and Needham.

'Yes, I can go, providing Sarah is available of course. But I'm going to be late getting there. Wasn't it ten o'clock you said the auctioneer was going to be there?'

He doesn't respond to this and looks as if his thoughts are miles away.

'Thank you. Here's the address.' He hands me a piece of paper.

'Not *Dove Cottage* then,' I remark after glancing at the address written on it. He either doesn't hear or doesn't think it funny, as he makes no comment. He usually picks up on my literary references, even when he's preoccupied or quite down. He gives me a weak smile and walks past me to re-enter the house.

'I've got to get some papers,' he says over his shoulder. 'See you tonight.'

I drive to Sarah's home. She's available, but doesn't get to the shop until almost ten. I promise to be back as soon as I can and set off for Grasmere.

Once I am on the road, I quickly forget about council meetings and being annoyed. Although the A591 is usually busy in summer, there is little traffic about on this crisp March morning and I am able to relax and enjoy the view. I love this stretch of road past Thirlmere, with the long narrow lake on my right and the thick woods on the left. Also somewhere to the left is the mighty Helvellyn, towering more than 3000 feet. But today I can hardly see past the top of the trees because of the mist and low clouds. Visibility improves as I reach the summit of Dunmail Raise, allowing me to enjoy the view of the valley ahead as I leave Cumberland behind and enter Westmorland to begin the descent into Grasmere.

I glance at my watch as I turn off the main road into the village. It shows ten forty-five. Grasmere is always busy. Its central location is ideal as a base for visitors to the Lakes District, and the village itself boasts a mile-long islet-dotted lake. But it is quite small, so I quickly locate the address.

It turns out to be a small slate-roofed cottage complete with a white picket fence and a neat English country garden. I am pleased to see only two cars parked outside, but my pleasure soon turns to dismay when a familiar figure comes walking out with what looks like a catalogue in his hand. He spots me as I get out of the car.

'Well well, the beautiful Emily Peel. Better late than never, I suppose. Where's John today? Couldn't he get himself out of bed?'

'He must have suspected you were going to be here, Phillip, and didn't want to upset his ulcers. Any luck inside?' I ask.

Phillip Scott owns a large antique store in Kendal, and we inevitably cross paths operating in the same area. John and he attended Keswick Grammar School at the same time and their friendly rivalry has existed since their schooldays. He has never married and usually flirts with me outrageously, but I have always thought it more to do with annoying John than him having any desire to attract me. I can see that he is empty handed, so consider my journey to be a waste of time.

'Nothing in there that I want,' he says. 'John probably got an anonymous tip the same as I did and just as probably sent out by the auctioneers to try to generate a few sales. New fellow inside, from Leeds. Didn't show a lot of enthusiasm. He must know it's a load of rubbish. It belonged to some old dear who passed away last month. The relatives must be trying to make a few quid out of it.'

'That a catalogue you have there?' I ask, nodding at the book in his hand.

'Not worth making up a catalogue for. This is a road map. I was just looking up the quickest way to my next port of call.'

'Another tip eh? Tell me the address. Maybe I can help you find the shortest route.'

'Nice try, Emily, but I didn't come down with the last shower. You find your own tips. You'll have to get up very early to catch me out. Have a look inside anyway, but I wouldn't expect too much help from the man in charge. I would guess he's new to the game.' Phillip tips his forelock to me, grins, and walks to his car.

I go inside the house. The two front rooms are very small and sparsely furnished, so I quickly find myself in a slightly larger room where the man in charge is seated at a small table. He looks very young and is busily writing in a notebook.

'Mind if I browse?' I ask.

'Help yourself,' he replies without looking up.

I take a quick look at the furniture before spotting a small shelf, with perhaps a dozen books on it. I walk over to it and see that they are quite dusty. Obviously Phillip hasn't considered them worthy of disturbing and after reading a few titles I can see why. They are old titles but they're reprints, so hardly rare.

The end one I recognise. It's one of my favourites from my schooldays, *Black Beauty* by Anna Sewell. I know it was first published in 1877, but when I look, I see that this copy is a far more recent print and some of the pages have been scribbled on with blue crayon. My eyes move along the shelf until I sight another copy of *Black Beauty*, this one with a dust cover. It must have been one of her favourites too, to own two copies.

I pick this one up to see if it is in better condition, with the possibility of buying it for sentimental reasons, and notice it's much thinner and feels lighter, and the cover doesn't fit properly. I glance towards the man in charge. He's still absorbed in his writing.

I slip the dustcover off and my experienced eyes see that the book inside is extremely old. The title reads: *Lyrical Poems, by William Wordsworth*, and it appears to be in good condition. I feel my heartbeat increase as I open the book. The first two pages are void of print, but one has a handwritten inscription: *To Caroline, on your eighth birthday, William*. My heart is racing as I turn the page.

Lyrical Poems
With
A few sketches.
Printed by Blackwall and Christian,
For S.W. Patterson, Cavendish St, London.
1798

I take a few deep breaths in an effort to slow down my racing heart and glance again at the young man, but his head is still down over his writing. The next page contains a printed list.

Contents
* Lines written in early spring
Too the cuckoo

The list is long, so I scan down it, to the end title.

Lines composed a few miles above Tintern Abbey.

I have myself under control by now. In fact, I am deadly calm.

I begin to carefully turn the pages, in deference to the pristine condition of the book. It looks genuine. Could I have stumbled across an original, printed in 1798? I will have to verify it, discreetly, but first I have to get it out of the building.

The thought that it now belongs to the family of the deceased and that the correct thing to do is to inform them of its existence does cross my mind; for a split second only. My dilemma over its being a valuable artefact that should be handed over to a museum or literary body for safekeeping, lasts only slightly longer. It will go to neither if I have my way.

It's more important to me as a tradeable commodity.

More thoughts cross my mind. Probably no one but me knows of its existence. The deceased woman must have concealed it with the *Black Beauty* cover for a reason. Perhaps she didn't like her next of kin. It doesn't really matter why. It'll be mine now if I can escape with it.

My quick wits have always enabled me to find a solution to my problems in the past, so my mind is working overtime. I decide to be brazen, in more ways than one. After all, he is a man, and young.

'Sorry to disturb you, but I'd like to buy this if it's not too dear. There are no price stickers on anything. How much is it?' I ask him, as I approach his table.

He doesn't look up immediately and keeps on writing. Then he sits back and looks at what he has written before turning his gaze towards me. He looks at my face at first and then his eyes wander down the gap made by my open coat, and then quickly back to my face. I haven't dressed for seduction, but I hope my sweater is tight enough to distract him.

'Sorry if I appeared to be ignoring you,' he says, 'but I have my auctioneers exams next week and I'm behind in my studies.'

'That's all right. I won't keep you long. You must have been as disappointed as I am with the contents of the house. But I saw this book, and as it was one of my favourites from my schooldays, I thought I would take it if it's not too expensive.' I hold the book in front of me so he can read the dust cover, and just below my breasts.

'*Black Beauty*, eh?' He reaches across the table and picks up a sheet of paper. 'Can't say I've read it. Here we are. Yes, there are two copies, according to this inventory.'

'Yes, there is one with crayon scribble on some of the pages. This one I've got appears to be clean. Are they priced?' One side of my coat is just about hanging off my shoulder. I hope I'm not overdoing it.

'If it was up to me you could have it. There's not much of a market for second-hand books, but I have to try and do the right thing by the deceased's family.'

Not much of a market for second hand books, eh? He's new alright.

'Are they local people?' I ask.

'No, they live in Somerset. The deceased and her parents moved here when she was very young. Name of Richardson. How does half a crown sound? Would you be willing to pay that?'

I look at him for a moment as if considering the price, before replying. 'Yes, that's all right, I don't want to do anyone out of their inheritance either.'

I open my handbag and take out my purse, all the time clutching the book. I hand him a half crown.

'Thank you, and good luck with your exams,' I say, and quickly turn to make my exit. I have only taken a few strides, however, when he calls out and my heart races again, thinking he wants to check the book.

'Sorry, but I will need your name for the receipt.'

Relieved, I say, 'Mary Jones.'

Chapter 26

There is a weak sun trying to break through the clouds as I return to my car and drive the short distance to *Dove Cottage*. This was William Wordsworth's home from 1799 to 1808 and the Wordsworth Trust has set up a museum here displaying a unique collection of manuscripts and books relating to the famous poet's work and life. Despite my eagerness to get inside I pause for a moment to admire the charming old two-story building. The Lake District has an abundance of historic houses and this one is an especially good example; it is made from local stone and its walls are white, lime washed to protect it from the damp. I have been inside before, so I know I'll be able to get a good idea of the authenticity of my find. It's still only eleven-twenty as I enter the museum, carrying the book. There are no other visitors, so it is quiet inside and the clatter of my feet on the slate floor startles the young woman behind a desk.

'Morning,' I say. 'Didn't expect to find you open on a week day this early in the year.'

'We probably shouldn't bother. I opened at ten and you're the only visitor so far. Do you require any help, or would you just like to take your time and look around.'

I notice she has a book open in front of her. She is probably eager to get back to it. 'I think I'll just look around. Mind if I take a few notes?'

'No go ahead.'

I part with another half crown for the entry donation, and consider it a worthy cause.

Casually wandering around the room, I stop at a glass-topped cabinet displaying a selection of letters written by Wordsworth. Pretending to be taking notes, I open my book and compare the inscription inside it with his writing in the letters. To my layman's eye, the handwriting and the signature match perfectly. So, William Wordsworth himself did inscribe this book. I move along to another cabinet and read where William and his sister Dorothy had moved from Dorset to Somerset in1797, to be nearer to Coleridge. I am getting quite excited by this time, thinking that the Somerset connection could explain how the old lady happened to have the book in her possession. I move to the next display. This contains material pertaining to his time in France, and his affair with Annette Vallon. There's not a lot to see, but one article holds my attention. It states that he left France in December 1792, before Vallon gave birth to his child Caroline. I believe for a moment that my heart actually stopped. The inscription in my book reads *To Caroline, on your eighth birthday, William*. All right, so it doesn't say 'Father' or 'Daddy', and I giggle out loud at the thought, or more likely it is to release some of the tension that has built up inside of me. I do a quick mental calculation. Caroline would have been born in 1793, which makes her eight years old in 1801, and my book was printed in 1798. It is possible that his daughter is the Caroline mentioned. There are no further mentions of Vallon or her daughter. Perhaps he did keep in touch with them but it was never recorded. I move to another case displaying books that are open at random pages. There it was. The plaque against one book read *Lyrical Poems*, and went on to say that this book was one of only three originals known to exist. One was in the British Museum and the other was last known to be in a private collection. I compare my book with the pages open in the display case. They are identical. Am I now in possession of the one in the private collection, or is this a fourth copy?

It is almost noon when I leave the museum. During visits to Grasmere I'd normally spend time at St Oswald's church where both Wordsworth and Coleridge are buried, or travel the extra few miles to Rydal to visit Rydal Mount where Wordsworth lived for over thirty years, but today all I look for is a public phone booth. I ring Sarah and apologise for taking so long and tell her I'm just leaving Grasmere and to lock up and put the *Closed for lunch* sign in the window. Sarah tells me that John has not put in an appearance. On the way home I park in a deserted picnic area near Lake Thirlmere and examine the book. I'm convinced it's genuine. I continue my drive home, anxious to discuss my find with John. I go to the shop first, find it closed, so continue on to the house and go inside. There's no indication that John has been back. I make myself a sandwich and return to the shop. The sun has disappeared behind the clouds and there are few people on the streets, so I'm not expecting much trade. I try to calm my frustration by tidying the shelves until four o'clock, before deciding to close for the day. John has still not returned when I get home. I've been keeping my find in my handbag all this time, being loath to let it out of my sight but realise I'll need to find a secure hiding place until I decide what to do with it. I don't consider the shop; too many people have access to it. I roam the house but can't see anywhere I consider safe. There's no alternative. I'll need to keep it with me at all times. The handbag I'm using barely conceals it and I don't have a bigger one. I'll have to buy a new one. It's still only four forty-five as I hurry to Main Street and the *Fashion Accessories and Leather Goods* shop. They're just about to close but I'm a good customer so the owner puts up the closed sign and helps me to find a suitable bag. One that's not so large as to attract attention but with a flat bottom. As I'm about to leave the shop I notice John's car parked further down the street, but on the other side. Next to it is the car Needham was driving this morning. I walk home and transfer the contents of my old handbag into the new one. My find sits flat on the bottom, well out of sight of any prying eyes whenever I have to open it.

I make a light meal for myself, as I'm not sure if John's council business includes dinner, as it often does. I watch the television for a while not taking in what is on, as my mind is busy recapping the day's events. It's after ten o'clock and I'm in bed but wide awake when John arrives home, the book tucked under my pillow.

He greets me with a weak smile.

'You've had a long day. You look exhausted. Have you eaten?' I ask. He's very pale. 'I saw your car parked next to Needham's earlier, fancy having to spend all day with him. What was so important as to take so much time?'

'I *am* exhausted, and yes, thank you, I have eaten. If you don't mind, I'll take one of my sleeping pills and try and get some rest. We can talk in the morning.'

'Too exhausted to hear about my finding a rare book,' I say, unable to contain myself.

'A rare book? I'm glad someone's had a good day.'

I'm surprised by his lack of enthusiasm but can control my excitement no longer. I pull the book out and hand it to him.

I watch eagerly, as he carefully turns the pages.

'This was in the house in Grasmere?' he asks.

'Yes, but concealed in the cover of another book. I virtually stole it.'

Before he can speak again, I blurt out the whole chapter of events, seeing Phillip, eluding the young auctioneer and checking its authenticity at *Dove Cottage*.

'My God, you did well! We'll have to have it valued.'

'Of course, eventually, but for now it'll have to be our secret. The old woman's family may find some reference to it and want to know what happened to it. Failing that, I doubt if anyone else is aware of its existence. It'll be ours to auction but we must never reveal how we've come to have it.'

'I'll have to find a safe hiding place for it.'

'Don't worry about that. I already have one.'

'Where?'

I am about to show him the handbag, when a vision of his cronies, Needham and Simpson, flashes through my mind. They would be the last people I would want to share a secret with.

'Best you don't know. You're not good with secrets, and there are a few of your associates I wouldn't want you telling, over a pint following a council meeting, say.'

'Well if you don't trust me, be like that. The responsibility will be all yours. This could be the chance of a lifetime.' He appears exasperated and his tone has taken on a sharp edge.

I tuck the book back under my pillow. He stands looking at me, as if wanting to continue the discussion, but I say, 'Goodnight John,' and turn away from him to sleep.

Chapter 27

I'm in a happy mood and hum a popular tune as I prepare to leave for the shop. Two weeks have passed since my find, and yesterday I attended the auction of the late Miss Richardson's estate and there was no mention of a missing book.

My relationship with John has been very strained. He's tried several times to persuade me to tell him where the book is hidden. He almost begged me last night when I returned from the auction and refused, saying it was still too soon. This morning he looks terrible. He's pale and has dark rings under his eyes, so I suggest he stays in bed and rests. The clouds that were hanging around yesterday have turned dark and it's beginning to drizzle. It is going to be another quiet day.

Having brought the newspaper from home, I make myself a cup of tea and sit down to read it. The headlines read: *England's second largest building company, goes broke.* The article takes up the whole of the front page, and profiles Sean Quigley, the young Irishman who had started laying bricks for a day wage, before forming his own building company in 1950. It says he built his reputation working in and around London but it was the motorway that made him a millionaire. He was one of the first to embrace this new initiative and visualise the need for cheap mass housing close to it. People would no longer have to live in the big cities and pay big city prices to be able to work there. The motorway would enable them to live further away and commute to work each day. Quigley had proceeded to purchase large tracts of land adjacent to the path of the motorway and had built housing estates, with affordable houses on them. Each house was the identical of its neighbour, so he was able to prefabricate his material and mass-produce them and in this way keep the price down. Brought up in a country of terrace houses, people had jumped at the chance to own a new semi-detached, with its own garden and often a garage, at a price they could afford. Quigley's became a household name as he followed the motorway north.

However, the report says, according to the experts, Quigley should not have insisted on it remaining a private company. He should have gone public, by floating it on the stock exchange. He pushed on too far. The suspension of the motorway's advance north while awaiting the construction of feeder roads meant that Quigley has built houses too far ahead of its progress and the wary public has not bought them fast enough. Quigley is unable to pay his creditors after getting himself too deeply into debt. He's declared himself bankrupt and faces criminal charges because he continued to sell houses that he knew would never be built.

I finish reading the article. It's another case of those that have being greedy and wanting more. It's only of passing interest, as I'm eager to flick through the pages for any reference to a missing rare book. I'm not looking forward to the motorway reaching Cumberland, making it all too easy for the masses from the big cities further south to make their way to the Lake District. It's overcrowded in summer now and I can't imagine what it will be like in four or five years' time. It might be better for business, but I have to live here as well.

A few coach parties arrive by the lake and the poor weather makes them head for the shops, so I'm busy for a while. I'm about to close for lunch, when a police sergeant in uniform and two men wearing dark suits enter. They don't look like customers.

'Mrs Peel? Mrs Emily Peel?' enquires the elder of the two men in suits.

'Yes,' I say.

He hands me a sheet of paper and a business card.

'This is a court order, empowering me to take possession of this shop and its contents.'

The card reads: *Grant & Mercer, Solicitors.* I begin to read the court order.

'I am required to ask you to hand over the keys to the shop and vacate the premises immediately.'

I don't acknowledge him until I've finished reading. It is as he says.

'I don't understand why you're doing this.'

'I was told that this would come as a shock to you, and I'm sorry. Your husband will explain. I can only suggest you go home and talk to him.' He speaks softly, and looks as if he is sorry.

I hand him the keys, pick up my handbag, and walk past my three visitors and into the street. I'm home in ten minutes.

John sits at the kitchen table. He had looked pale when I left for the shop this morning but now all the blood seems to have drained from his face, and his eyes are red, as if he's been crying. He looks towards me but doesn't make eye contact.

'What's going on, John? A solicitor has taken over the shop.'

I place the court order on the table in front of him as I say it. He doesn't look at it and hands me a similar looking document.

'I've been very unlucky, Emily.'

'Unlucky?'

'Have you read the paper yet?'

'Yes, but what has that got to do with it?'

'Quigleys'. I invested money in them and now it's all gone.'

'What money? How much? Where did you get it?'

'Money I borrowed from the bank. Twenty thousand pounds.'

I'm speechless for a moment then the impact of what he has just said sinks in and I collapse onto a chair opposite him.

'Start from the beginning. Why would the bank lend you that much? We only just managed to get the mortgage.'

'It started about six months ago. We were having a drink in the Royal Oak, after a council meeting. We, being Needham, Simpson, and Dr Patel from the hospital. They told me how Quigleys' operated and said that they were getting a syndicate together to buy into a development that was planned for Penrith. They asked me if I was interested. They made it all sound so easy and the profit was to be astronomical.'

I had a few questions but let him continue.

'I said it sounded all right, but when they mentioned the amount of money each syndicate member would have to put up, I told them I didn't have that sort of money. That's when Simpson and Needham produced the new valuation of our house and told me what the shop was worth. Simpson said he would loan me the money using the house and shop as collateral. Not that we own that much of the house yet.'

I look at the paper he has handed me. It is a court order seizing the house.

'Let me get this straight,' I say. 'You used the house and shop as collateral to get a loan of twenty thousand pounds, to invest in a property deal. Now the building company has gone broke and you've lost it all? We've no house or business.'

He looks at the floor when he answers. 'That's exactly it. I'm so sorry, Emily. It all sounded so simple. It was bad luck the developer going broke.'

'Bad luck doesn't come into it. Bloody stupidity is how I'd describe it. Wait a minute though; I'm part owner of the house. Surely they can't take my half too. I wasn't part of the syndicate.'

He starts to cry, deep gasping sobs. 'Yes you were. I'm sorry. The document you signed agreeing to the extra payments on the mortgage, was actually the syndicate contract.'

That really floors me and I sit there stunned. My mind is in a state of utter confusion. How can it have all gone so quickly? We had everything going for us. A lovely home, a successful business, we were respected members of the community. Now John has let me down. He tricked me into blindly signing a document that has led to our financial ruin.

I struggle to restrain myself from physically attacking him. He would probably have welcomed it. He'll be expecting some reaction, some excuse for more self-pity. What a pathetic creature he is. Successful business or not, how could I have married such a person? What was that expression, 'hoisted by your own petard'? I had grabbed at the first opportunity of easy money and now I am paying for it. He's so weak. I should have been warned when he told me of Penny tormenting him; instead, I decided to help him. I gave him back his manhood, his dignity, and he's rewarded me by fawning over the likes of Simpson and Needham. I bet they haven't lost everything. They will have hedged their bets somehow.

I fight to regain my composure. I remember the book I have in my handbag. No wonder he's been so persistent with his search for it. Now I know why. He would have tried for a quick sale, selling it under value in order to clear his debts before they became public knowledge. The book's worth a small fortune if I can find a way to convert it into money. And after what he's just done, I'll see that he doesn't get his hands on any of it. That's for sure.

'This news answers a lot of questions. Now I know why you're after my book. You've really complicated things now, John. Just when it looked as if we were in the clear as far as the Richardson family's claim to it is concerned, we have to contend with Grant & Mercer confiscating it as part of the shop stock. I keep saying 'we', but believe me, I mean me. And I'll now need to be able to prove that it came into my possession after you lost the shop. What are we going to do? Do we have to vacate the house today too?'

He looks me in the eye for the first time and says wearily. 'I don't know what we're going to do. There was no council meeting yesterday. We were locked up with the solicitors all day. Unlike the shop, we're allowed to stay in the house until it's sold, providing we don't remove anything.'

'Small consolation that is and by 'don't remove anything', I take it that we have lost all the antiques as well? It has taken almost six years to accumulate them. I can't forgive you for this, John and I can't bear to be in your presence just now. I'll go and spend the rest of the day with my mother. I suppose it's still all right to drive my car. She'd better hear this from me, before anyone else finds out. You can sit here, wallowing in self-pity and thinking about what you're going to do with the rest of your life. And whatever you decide, don't include me in it.'

'What about the book? We could eventually sell it and make a fresh start.'

'Forget about the book. As far as you're concerned, it doesn't exist.'

Chapter 28

The drive to Workington is a blur. The events of the past twenty-four hours occupy my mind.

Mother sits in silence for a while when I tell her.

'I can hardly believe it,' she finally says. 'I considered John to be a very sensible young man. I can't offer a reason why these things occur. You know what I mean; circumstances changing that are beyond our control. Like my having to leave the Oldfields' in Oldham and then the Watsons'. But in return I gained you and through you wanting to be a librarian I found Peter. Now this has happened to you.' Then she smiles. 'I wonder what fate is going to bring you in return, Emily?'

Peter comes home and is equally shocked.

'I don't know what to say other than to let you know that you're welcome to stay here as long as you like. We'll do whatever we can to help you.'

'Thank you. That's very kind. I have no idea what I'm going to do. It'll take a while for all this to sink in. One day I have a house and a thriving business and the next day it's gone. It's nice to know I have you two to rely on though. It's too early to make any long-term plans but I'll stay for a few nights before I go and collect my clothes. There's no way I'm going to live in the house with John until it's sold.'

Peter and I watch the TV news while my mother prepares dinner. It has the Quigleys' collapse as its lead story and tells how hundreds of people across the country have lost thousands of pounds as a result. I feel no better knowing John's only one of a few hundred who have lost money.

Mother's cooking is as delicious as ever, but I have little appetite. I'm too distraught.

Peter tries to ease the sombre mood. As Mother hands me a cup of tea, he catches my eye and winks, then turns to my mother.

'Well Ruth, I don't know about you, but I think this is fate's way of giving Emily another opportunity to become a librarian.'

She looks from him to me, notices we are both smiling and begins to smile herself.

'You can laugh if you want, but everything that happens is for a reason. For every problem there's a solution.'

I agree wholeheartedly. I just have to find one for this particular problem.

The unfamiliar bed is not what keeps me awake. Nor is the loss of practically everything I ever owned. I have almost got over the shock and disbelief. I think how strange it is that Quigleys' collapse has occurred after I found the book and showed it to John. How fortunate I am to have found that book. No one needs to know about the timing or how I came to have it. But why did I have to show it to John? Big mistake. I'd feel a lot easier if he knew nothing about it. I'm more than ever determined to conceal its existence. After all, it's only mine because of possession. It belongs to the old woman's heirs, even though they don't know about it and I still have to find a way to own it legitimately.

Chapter 29

On the second morning of my stay Peter leaves for work and I stand up to clear away the breakfast dishes.

Mother sits back in her chair and is staring at a place somewhere above my head.

'Leave that for now Emily,' she says.

I sit down again.

'I never did get round to telling you why I married your father did I?' she says.

I sit back in my chair now, all ears.

'First you have to understand the situation we were in,' she says. 'We had been living like a family after Mrs Watson died. By we I mean Mr Watson and George and me. Although I went home to my mother's every evening, I made all of their meals, did the washing and household chores as well as keep the books for the business. I was happy. I had lived in Jane's shadow all my life. I loved her, but whatever I had achieved I had done so with her guidance. Then she married Bob and stayed in Oldham and I found myself on my own for the first time in my life.

'I was like a lost soul for a while. Then came the Watson situation. It was the first time I had done anything without Jane and I had made a success of it. Then almost overnight it was gone. Mr Watson sold the business, George lost his job and I went back to living with my mother.'

A bit like my present situation, I think.

She continues. 'I admit to being a bit of a dreamer. I only ever see the good side of anyone or anything, as if life is a fairy story and will always have a happy ending. I had to learn the hard way that it wasn't so.

'I felt sorry for George from the moment I met him. To me he was like a giant puppy dog, always friendly but always needing someone to look after him. I decided to improve his life. I began to teach him things so he would understand the world around him better. But it was all one way. It made me feel good, doing what I was trying to do for him, but I don't think he even realised what I was doing. He was happy as he was and I couldn't see it, couldn't see that I was really doing it for my own benefit.'

She stops talking. Then her eyes meet mine.

'The day George found out he had lost his job and would soon be out of a home must have been one of the worst days of his life. He stormed out of the house without a word to either Mr Watson or me. I heard later that he had been drinking heavily. Heavier than usual I mean He got really drunk. He even threatened to punch Alec. I was worried about his state of mind, so I stayed in the Watsons' house waiting for him to come home. It rained heavily that night and he came home drunk and sopping wet. He was hardly able to stand, so I began to help him off with his wet clothes. I was concerned about him catching his death of cold.'

Mother takes a sip of the remaining tea that had gone cold in her cup.

'He fell onto the floor and I was dragged down with him. The next thing I knew he was on top of me and my skirt was up around my neck. Then he was inside of me. It all happened so quickly. I protested but he was too strong and too heavy. I couldn't get away or stop him. I honestly don't think he knew what he was doing. Then he rolled off me and fell asleep. I cleaned myself up and left him there snoring his head off.'

I cross the narrow space between us and put my arms around her.

'You don't have to tell me anymore, Mother,' I say. I feel guilty for ever having asked her.

She continues as if she hadn't heard me; as if unburdening herself of her secret was going to somehow make it less painful.

'I never saw Mr Watson again until your father's funeral. Your father found a job at the steelworks and lived in lodgings in Moss Bay. I was determined not to see him again and began to look for work. Two months later I discovered I was pregnant. My mother heard me retching a few mornings and we had a row. She said I was bringing disgrace to the family by carrying on with a drunken oaf. She made it sound like I was a slut. I knew I had to leave. But I had no money no chance of working and would soon have a baby to look after.

'I was still dreaming of a happy ending even then. I decided I could recreate the situation we had at the Watsons'. I would marry George. We would rent a house, he would go to work and I would look after him and the baby. Alec had helped your father find a job and digs so I got him to come with me to see your father.

'We were married soon after. As you know the baby died. A pneumonia epidemic swept the country and both the baby and I were affected. I was sick for a long time and if it hadn't have been for Jane I would probably have died too.

'Jane wanted me to leave your father and go to live in Oldham. I thought about it. But Jane and Bob were just beginning to get ahead and I didn't want to be a burden on them, so I decided I would stay with your father long enough to save enough money to be able to support myself. But your father changed. Almost overnight he began to drink more. His work suffered. He had an accident. One day he forgot to wear his gaiters and a shower of sparks flew into his boots when he dropped a red-hot rail. I think that made him realise that despite his size and strength he was no different from any other man.

'That's when the beatings started. He would come home drunk and take his frustration out on me. I was pregnant with you by then and had nowhere else to go again. So I stayed.'

'That's filled in a lot of gaps from what Aunt Jane has told me. But why have you never told *her* what happened?' I ask.

'There's another thing I am ashamed of. At the same time I found out I was pregnant the first time, I received a letter from Jane in which she told me how well she and Bob were doing but how disappointed she was that she had not been able to get pregnant. As I mentioned before, Jane had always had a hand in whatever I had achieved. All this time I had been envious of Jane and her ideal husband, their nice house and thriving business and now I had achieved something Jane could not do although she wanted it badly, that is to get pregnant. It made me want the baby more than ever and I think it blinded me to a lot of faults in my grand plan to marry George.

'I have felt unworthy of having a sister like Jane ever since. I could never tell her. And I blame myself for putting you through the poverty stricken life we led when you were growing up. I was never a strong person like Jane. She wouldn't have put up with what I did. I often wished George dead but that was as far as it got, wishing. You are more like Jane than like me. I hope my weakness didn't contribute to your present situation.'

We sit in silence for a while. I think about what she has just said. About her thinking of killing my father and about me being strong like Aunt Jane. Did that mean she knows I killed him? I could never ask her outright.

We have a lot in common. We both started out by trying to help a man to improve his life. We both married men out of convenience rather than love. Manipulative bitches, the two of us.

'No Mother, nothing you did was responsible for what happened to me. We each make our own way in the world. Along the way there are decisions to be made, decisions that decide our future. We make the right one and life is a bed of roses; we make the wrong one and life is a bed full of weeds. But all is not lost. There are plenty more decisions to be made.'

**

Later that day I have had enough of being indoors moping around. I get in my car and set off with no particular destination in mind. I just want to be alone for a while. Although it was not a conscious decision I find myself in Keswick. There must be something about this town that draws me to it. I park my car and wander around Fitz Park before coming to rest on a park bench. I stare at the people playing Mini-Golf but do not see them; my mind is elsewhere.

As usual it is the book that occupies my thoughts. I sit and ponder the folly of my telling John. I will need to convince him not to tell anyone about it. My future could depend on his keeping my secret. It's going to be difficult; since I told him he had no further claim on it. What to do, what to do?

Chapter 30

It's been three days since I left John. I still have no idea of what I'm going to do in the future. But I do need to go and collect my clothes. I feel sick at the thought of returning to the house; at the thought of seeing John again. I know I can't just keep putting it off. The more I do, the longer I go on dreading the moment. So I rise early, and after a quick breakfast I set off for Keswick. I park behind John's car. I walk up to the house, slip my key in the lock and open the door.

It's quiet inside, with no television or radio noise. I go upstairs to our bedroom.

I lower my suitcase down from the top of the wardrobe and begin to pack it. I hadn't realised I had accumulated so many clothes. I will never get everything in and I'm certainly not coming back. The larger items will have to lie on the back seat. I go to the bathroom to collect my toiletries.

John's in the bath. He's lying fully clothed and face down in the red coloured water. There's the sweet, sickly smell of blood. His arm feels cold and stiff when I touch it. The bathroom stool is overturned. I right it and slump down. The little two-bar electric heater is on and the room is uncomfortably hot. Blood has congealed on one of the taps. The taps are large and ornate. We chose the old bath because of the taps. I'll need to phone the police. I go downstairs to the hallway.

As I reach the bottom of the stairs the doorbell rings. I automatically open the door. The younger of the two solicitors I had last seen in the shop stands before me.

'Sorry to disturb you so early Mrs Peel, but we have some prospective buyers who wish to look through the house. Would it be convenient to show them through at ten o'clock?' he says.

I run a hand through my hair and stare at him, not comprehending his words.

'Are you all right?' he asks. 'You look very pale,'

'I've just arrived home and found my husband dead in the bathtub.'

He takes my arm and leads me into the kitchen. I sit down at the table.

'Have you phoned the police?'

I shake my head.

'Wait there, I'll do it.'

He leaves the room and I hear his footsteps on the stairs. He comes back down and I hear him on the phone.

'They'll be here soon. Would you like me to make you a cup of tea while we're waiting? You must have had a terrible shock.'

I shake my head again.

Twenty minutes later, two uniformed policemen and a man wearing a dark suit and carrying a small black leather bag arrive. One of the policemen and the man in the suit go upstairs. The other policeman comes and sits next to me.

'I'm Sergeant Carter,' he says. 'This must have been a shock to you. Are you up to answering a few questions?'

'Yes, I think so.'

'You told the solicitor that you had just arrived home and found your husband dead in the bath. Could you tell me where you'd been?'

'I've been sleeping at my mother's house in Workington for a few nights.'

He asks the address and if there is a phone. I tell him and he writes in a notebook.

'And what time did you get home this morning?'

'About seven thirty.'

The other policeman comes downstairs and stands in the kitchen doorway. Sergeant Carter walks over to him and shows him what he has written in his notebook.

'Sorry to have to ask you these questions at such a time Mrs Peel. I'm Inspector Underwood. There's a suitcase packed with clothes on the bed upstairs. Were you going away?' the other policeman asks.

'I was going to stay with my mother for a while. We have to vacate the house.'

The young solicitor walks over to join the two policemen and begins to speak to them in a voice too low for me to hear. The inspector nods several times.

'When did you last see your husband alive, Mrs Peel?'

'Three days ago he was here when I left to go to my mother's.'

'Sorry again to have to ask you this but you went on your own and now the suitcase. Did you and your husband have words, I mean, a disagreement perhaps?'

I assume he has just been told about our losing the shop and house. 'Yes, I was upset. I'd just found out he'd made a bad investment and lost all our money.'

The sergeant wrote it all down. The man in the suit came to join them. They move out of the kitchen as he begins to speak. I can't hear what they are saying but they keep looking at me as he speaks. They leave the house, except for the inspector, who returns to the kitchen.

'That will be all for now Mrs Peel. Dr Williams will arrange for the removal of your husband's body. I don't know if you are aware but when a death is not due to natural causes there is usually an inquest, conducted by the coroner. It's just a formality really. Although he can call witnesses, it's not like a trial; it's only to enable him to determine the cause of death so he can issue a death certificate. It's nothing for you to be concerned about. As you were previously planning to stay with your mother, I would suggest that you still do. Do you require any immediate assistance? Do you feel capable of driving yourself to Workington? Is there anyone you would like me to call or speak to on your behalf?'

I feel weak and suddenly tired, but want to be alone more than anything else. 'Thank you, Inspector; I'm a little shaken up by what has happened. I don't just mean today, but losing everything as well. I'll be all right. I'll just sit here for a while and then phone my mother. The house is in the hands of the solicitors now, so they can take care of it. I will lock it when I leave and drop my keys through the letterbox. They already have keys to the shop and the house.'

'Goodbye for now then,' he says. 'We have your mother's address and phone number, so we will let you know the date and time of the inquest. You can bring her with you if you want.'

I phone my mother after he has gone and by the time I've brought my clothes downstairs Peter has called to say he's getting a colleague to drive him to Keswick so that he can drive my car back. I argue that I'll be all right but he insists and I'm pleased, because all my energy has drained out of me and I really don't feel up to driving.

Chapter 31

Both my mother and Peter come with me to the inquest. The coroner does call witnesses and it appears to be as the inspector said, just a formality. As I expected it to be having attended Penny's inquest, everyone simply states the facts.

I'm called first, having discovered the body. I tell it exactly as I told Sergeant Carter. The second witness is the young solicitor, called because he was the one who reported the incident. They don't refer to it as an accident at this stage. Sergeant Carter is next and reads from his notebook, confirming that what I've just said is what I told him.

I feel relaxed before and during the proceedings, until Dr Williams, the man in the suit begins to speak. He speaks in a monotone voice, which drones on for about five minutes before I begin to realise how serious this business is.

He tells how he had examined the body at the scene and found a gash on John's forehead, which was consistent with someone having fallen onto the tap. He says lividity was fixed, enabling him to determine that the body had not been moved after death. He says a post-mortem examination has revealed water in the lungs, consistent with that in the bath, confirming he was alive when he entered the water and that drowning was the cause of death.

A urine sample has revealed traces of sleeping powder, consistent with the sleeping tablets found in the bathroom cabinet. A Dr Patel prescribed the tablets for the deceased. The body was in full rigor, showing he had been dead longer than twelve hours, but how much longer was difficult to tell.

He says calculating the exact time of death is complicated. The water in the bath would have been hot, and he found a two-bar electric heater burning, apparently for a long time. It was probably lit by the deceased, making the small room very warm, which would have slowed down the normal body cooling process. The stomach contents revealed he had eaten very little during the previous twenty-four hours, so the digestion process was of no help in determining the time of death.

Dr Williams concludes by saying he had first sighted the body at eight ten am and considers that death could have occurred anytime between three pm and eight pm the previous day.

The coroner thanks everyone for attending and announces that based on the evidence presented to him he'll return a verdict of accidental death.

I am pleased when it is finally over.

An aunt of John's, whom I have never met, introduces herself and asks if he can be buried in the family plot in Ambleside, alongside his parents. I tell her that he has lost all our money and that I will have to borrow money to pay for his funeral. The aunt tells me that she will be happy to pay for it, as well as make all the arrangements. We sign the necessary forms there and then and I tell her I will not be attending the funeral.

As we are leaving, I notice Phillip Scott getting into his car. He catches my eye and nods but I ignore him. My mother and Peter's presence must have kept him from approaching me. I had noticed him earlier inside, sitting in the public area. John and he must have been better friends than I had thought for him to attend the inquest. Thank goodness I am no longer involved in the antique trade and will not have to associate him anymore.

Chapter 32

It takes me longer than I expect to get over the loss of the house and business and John's death.

I'm glad to settle down in Workington once more and in the relative luxury of my mother's new home. I pay a visit to Iris and spend a few quiet minutes of reflection while gazing at the small blocks of flats built on the site where we once lived. I don't tell my mother, because we never mention the past.

I start working part-time in the Workington branch of Cartwrights' to earn some money while I ponder my future. The irony of this turn in my career is not lost on me.

I don't have to consider John now when I think about the book in my bag but I still haven't found a way to lawfully claim it as mine.

For the first time since I was a child, I am without a plan. I took my chance and escaped from poverty. I acquired a husband, a successful business and a fine house in a sought-after neighbourhood. I became someone. I had a standing in society. Now what I had has gone and I'll have to start all over again. I can't begin to see how it can get worse.

Workington is well blessed with open space. There are two large parks. Vulcan Park easily accessed from the centre of town and adjacent to the Grammar School, so I know it well. It's very formal and set out with neat pathways dividing lawns and flowerbeds, and boasting a bandstand. My favourite though is Curwen Park, the larger of the two and situated on the outskirts of town. It's a large field with a narrow stream running through a small wooded area in one corner and a scattering of football and rugby pitches available to the public. Next to this is the Mill Field, another large grassed area often filled with grazing cows with the broad River Derwent running down one side attracting the local salmon fishermen.

I like living in Elizabeth Street. Park End Road runs along the top of it, and from there it is only a short walk to Curwen Park and Workington Hall, a large quadrangular building now in ruins. I have visited the Museum, in a nearby eighteenth-century house and have seen a full-scale model of the hall intact and there is sufficient of it left to allow me to imagine it in its prime. I draw comfort from its longevity, from knowing it has been there since the fourteenth century, and has played its part in the country's history. The Curwen family lived in Workington from the year 1250 and in the hall until 1929. Mary Queen of Scots spent her last day of freedom there in 1568. Henry Curwen was an infamous Jacobite Rebel and John Christian Curwen was a cousin of Fletcher Christian, famous for his part in the mutiny on the Bounty.

When I visit the museum and look at the model of the hall and when I visit what remains of Workington Hall itself, I feel that I too can survive.

I've adopted the habit of eating my lunch here, sitting on a wooden bench and gazing through the trees towards the park. It's quiet during the week, which leaves me undisturbed. I enjoy having the place largely to myself.

I breathe in the air. I love the quality of the light in the middle of the day at this time of the year, especially if the sky is clear. I appreciate having time and space to sit and think.

Chapter 33

A few weeks have passed since the inquest into John's death. I'm on my lunch break from Cartwrights'. The sky is overcast but no rain as yet so I head for the Workington Hall ruin and claim my favourite bench.

Shortly after I observe a tall man wearing a grey raincoat walking down the path towards me. As he draws nearer, I can see he isn't young but carries himself well, with a military-like bearing. I'm expecting him to walk on by and prepare myself to exchange casual greetings with him, if he should speak, when he veers off the path, walks the few steps over the grass and sits on the bench beside me. Although he looks vaguely familiar, I can't immediately place him.

'Good afternoon Emily, do you remember me?

I look hard at him. Then it dawns on me. It is the police sergeant who took my statement at the scene of Penny's accident.

'Yes, I do now. It's Sergeant Outhwaite isn't it? The civilian clothes fooled me. Are you still in Keswick, or have you retired?'

'You've a good memory for names, Emily. Actually it's Detective Sergeant Outhwaite now and I'm based in Carlisle, but the long arm of the law knows no boundaries, so I travel about a bit. I'd like to have a little chat with you, all unofficial like, you understand.'

'So this isn't a chance encounter then?'

He smiles at me. 'No, I knew you'd be here and I'd like to relate a conversation I had recently with my Superintendent.'

I feel rather apprehensive but make no comment, so he continues.

'I told him I knew a young woman called Emily, who seemed to attract accidents. I told him I'd first met her when her father fell down a flight of stairs and broke his neck. Although I said "fell", I also mentioned that at the time we felt it strange that he had climbed the stairs in the dark when the light was working, so I asked him to consider that he may have been pushed.'

This is the last thing I expect. What's coming next? I open my mouth to protest at this suggestion but he raises his hand.

'Hear me out first, please. Then you can have your say.'

'My Super said, "What would have been the motive?" I suggested that as he was known to be a rough character, he may have been a wife and daughter beater, and got his just deserts. I then told him about this same Emily coming across a woman who'd fallen into a stream and drowned, a woman who just happened to be the wife of her employer, whom she later married.'

This is too much; I can contain myself no longer. 'As I recall, your constable confirmed at the inquest that the bike tyre tracks at the scene showed we came from opposite directions.'

The detective sergeant meets my eyes with a level gaze and smiles. 'That's true, but he also said that the snow around the area where she apparently went over the bridge was roughed up. And, though the gash on her forehead was consistent with her having hit her head on the top of the wall where we found traces of her hair and blood, this doesn't prove that she fell into the water. She could have been sufficiently stunned by the knock to allow someone to heave her over the wall.

'I only mentioned these two coincidences to him after I had found a third. As a matter of procedure, copies of files recording deaths that require a coroner's inquest are passed on to the police.

'I happened to be in Keswick on another case and heard about the accidental drowning of a man called John Peel. My curiosity was aroused because he had the same name as the famous huntsman, so I had a glance at his file. I read where his widow's name was Emily, and it didn't take a great deal of detective work to discover that her maiden name was Wilson.

'He's very big on motives, my Super. So by this time he was looking very interested. He said, "So you're suggesting that this Emily Wilson is some sort of serial killer? That she may have pushed her father down the stairs even though she was a child, and was responsible for the death of the Peel woman, her motive being to enable her to marry the husband, whom she also killed?"

'I agreed. Then I pointed out that in John Peel's case, the time of death was very vague and fixed sometime between three pm and eight pm the previous day. And although Emily Peel had said she last saw him alive three days previously, she had confessed to being upset at her husband losing all their money, and she had been packing as if to leave him.

'So, it was possible for her to have returned and killed him. To have hit him on the head, knocking him unconscious, or making him dazed. It would have then been easy for her to bang his head against the tap, on the same spot, and to hold him under the water until he drowned, before returning to her mother's to establish an alibi.

'In addition, don't forget, he would have already been groggy with the sleeping tablet. That he either took himself, or had given to him without his knowledge, by having it dissolved in a drink of some sort. My Super was really excited by now. But then he spoiled it by asking me her motive.

'I had already told him they had lost all their money and property, and as yet no insurance policy had turned up, and there didn't appear to be a lover in the picture, so I couldn't answer that one.

'Other than to suggest she did it for revenge, this Emily had nothing to gain from killing him. So, I was told to forget about these coincidences and get on with my other cases.' He pauses for effect, and looks intently at me, 'Unless of course something turns up in the future.'

For a long moment I can't speak. My mouth is so dry that my tongue is sticking to the roof. I try to remain calm.

'That's an interesting story, Detective Sergeant, and very entertaining, but I think you have an overactive imagination. You've hardly got a smoking gun and wouldn't the post-mortem examination have revealed he had received two blows to the head, even though they were in the same spot?

'You're well informed, Emily. You must read a lot of those detective novels you sell. You're right of course. But from my reading of the report, it would appear that the examiner had already assumed the death to be an accident and didn't feel it necessary to waste time looking for signs of foul play. Of course, as the body was buried and not cremated, it could be exhumed for a more thorough examination. That is, if a motive was to suddenly appear.'

'Is there anything else, Detective Sergeant? I seem to have lost my sense of humour. Would you like a sandwich? I seem to have lost my appetite as well.'

'No, nothing else for now, Emily. As I said, this is all unofficial.' He stands up, and continues on his way down the path.

I'm very disturbed by what he has said and try not to panic, but find it difficult to breath, as if there's a band tightening round my chest, and I realise I've been tensing every muscle in my body. I remember telling my mother that people get what they deserve in this world. Was my past sin catching up with me? Was my father reaching out from the grave to get his revenge? What if they do exhume the body and do find two blows to the head? Then it dawns on me and I laugh out loud. There's no evidence to link me to John's death, so why would they exhume the body? Why would

John be in the bath with his clothes on if he hadn't fallen while preparing to take a bath? John looked as if he'd fallen and hit his head on the tap. This is what the doctor said. The coroner said accidental death. End of story. No one but Detective Sergeant Outhwaite has suggested I have done anything wrong. It's strange how the mind plays tricks when the conscience isn't clear. But I can't completely relax, I hadn't considered anyone would think John's death was anything but an accident and yet this man has been discussing me with his superior officer. He's been making enquiries about me, he knew my movements, knew I would be on that bench. Who has he talked to? I'll be viewing everyone with suspicion for the next few days. I think about the book in my handbag. The handbag that's been sitting on the bench between us as we talked. I am sure he'd see that and the fact I was concealing its existence as being ample motive.

Chapter 34

The book and how to make use of it has completely taken over my life, I think of little else. I'll need to manufacture proof that I discovered it after John's death. Not only to satisfy Sergeant Outhwaite, but also Grant & Mercer. That is, if the truth doesn't reveal itself, allowing the legitimate owners to claim it first. I realise I'm caught up in a tangled web and know I'll soon have to deceive a lot of people.

My deliberations are interrupted temporarily when I receive a chatty note from Alicia, inviting me to come to booze up in the Grey Mare, in celebration of her thirtieth birthday. I'm not in the best frame of mind to be in the midst of a crowd of happy people but feel I should attend, if only to please the one remaining friend I have.

I borrow Peter's car for the journey but make the mistake of arriving late, about nine o'clock. There's nothing worse at a party than to be the only completely sober person there. They must have started early, as the party is in full swing. I make my way through the crowd towards the bar. I feel very much out of place. Why does everyone look so young? How come I can't see any familiar faces? I've spent a lot of happy evenings in this room, but it was a long time ago and the old crowd must have moved on. Those carefree days were interrupted by dreams of being married and owning a successful business. If I were to be honest with myself I might own up to having once joined the ranks of those who had wealth, position and success, but wanted more.

I finally see Alicia. She's standing with a drink in each hand, between two good-looking young men. They each have an arm around her, one of them far enough to have a hand on her breast. At least some things never change, I think, although these two look barely old enough to interest her.

Alicia spots me and bursts free of the two men. She hands me one of her drinks and gives me a squeeze with her free arm. 'Glad you came, Emily. I must be getting old. I don't get the same enjoyment out of parties anymore.'

'You could have fooled me. You look like you're doing all right.'

'Oh, those two? No idea who they are. Far too young for my tastes. I think they're trying to get me boozed so they can have their evil way with me.'

'Boy, are they in for a shock.'

Alicia laughs out loud before her face takes on a more serious look. 'You don't look well, Em. Still not got over John's death?'

'I suppose that's part of my problem. I just can't seem to be able to move on. And I'm also too old for this sort of thing,' I say, waving my arm around the room.

Just then, a man whose face I know but can't put a name too, comes and puts his arm around Alicia and she turns towards him and gives him a peck on the cheek. I sip my drink and pull a face. Alicia was right about the two young men. The drink was at least a triple gin, with barely a splash of tonic.

'Well well, this is opportune. I was about to get in touch with you and here you are, painting the town red. Not letting the grass grow under your pretty feet, eh? I haven't seen you for a while, Emily. You look great.'

I turn to greet Phillip Scott.

'Another thing that hasn't changed: flattery will get you nowhere, Phillip.' I knew I didn't look great.

'You're a long way from home so late in the day, Phillip. Not many antiques in here, none that are for sale anyway.'

'Lots of places close by to visit tomorrow though, so I thought I'd stay overnight at the Royal Oak and get an early start in the morning.'

'How's business? You don't have to conceal your tip-offs from me anymore, so you can be honest for a change.'

'Ha ha, very funny! Business is good. Lots of old people dying these days, and their heirs just want to sell with no thought to the future. Lots of bargains around, and that's what I want to discuss with you.'

Lots of bargains around for someone as unscrupulous as you, I think, but don't say.

'Why would you want to discuss anything with me? I'm out of the game now, with nothing to show for it.'

He smiles that leering smile of his and taps the side of his nose with his finger, in a gesture designed to let me know he considers I have something to hide and that we share a secret.

I immediately think of the book, but decide he can't possibly know about that. It really is going to be difficult to sell though without raising too many eyebrows. Everyone in the game is on the lookout for the once in a lifetime opportunity of a rare find. There'll be a lot of questions asked if I ever reveal the book's existence.

Alicia returns and obviously doesn't like Phillip, as she gives him a fierce glare. He feigns shock by holding his hands in front of him palms up and moves away.

'That man gives me the creeps. He spent one night in here giving me a few sneaky gropes, so I told him I thought he'd be able to walk under a snake's belly wearing a top hat and he's ignored me ever since.'

Alicia can always make me laugh and this time she's also saved me from further interrogation.

We dump our drinks, buy two halves of bitter beer and toast Alicia's birthday. I don't get time for a long conversation, as my friend's in big demand, with well-wishers turning up throughout the evening. I bid her farewell shortly after ten and fight my way through the crowd to the door.

Because I arrived late, I had to park down a side street away from the pub, as the car park was full. I'm about to unlock the car when a hand grabs my arm and a man's body presses me against the door. I am too startled to scream, and before I have time to recover, his hands pin my arms behind my back. I feel Phillip's mouth brushing against my ear.

'I wasn't kidding, Emily. I know you have something, so let me have a look to see what it might be worth.'

'Get away from me, Phillip. You know nothing. We lost everything.'

He twists my arm up further behind my back.

'I don't want to hurt you, Emily, but if I have to I will. John told me about your find and how you came by it. He asked me to discreetly get an estimate of its value and if I knew of any buyers who would be willing to pay cash, in exchange for a reduced price. Give it to me and you'll never have to see me again.'

My mind is in a state of chaos, I was right in thinking that John would have disposed of it cheaply to make a quick sale, but had never considered he would tell anyone like Phillip about it.

'Let go of my arm. You're hurting me already, and you're the last person I would give it too.'

'Now you're being foolish. The book is no longer of any value to you. If you try to sell it, I'll expose you as a thief and a possible murderess. We can even work together. I'm willing to share the proceeds with you and I have the contacts.

'There are private buyers who would be willing to pay cash, with no questions asked. It need never see the light of day again, and we'd both make money.

'You wouldn't want to go the same way as your husband, would you? That would serve no purpose. You wouldn't benefit if you had an accident before you revealed where you've hidden the book. It was unfortunate for John that I didn't believe him when he said he didn't know where it was.

'You know, I've always fancied you, Emily. This could be the start of a beautiful friendship.'

Phillip thrusts his groin between my buttocks to emphasise what he's just said, then presses his body closer so that my left arm stays pinned when his hand lets go of it. He jerks my right arm higher behind my back.

'I'll have those keys, thank you, Emily, and don't think I won't break your arm if I have to.'

I let the keys go and he quickly pockets them, pressing closer while sliding round my left buttock and wrapping his left arm under my breasts so that my left arm still stays pinned and he can take a firm hold of my right. This enables him to free his right arm while still constraining mine, now that he no longer feels the need to twist it higher behind my back and threaten to break it.

Phillip's right hand lets go of my right arm and moves down my side, coming to rest on my thigh. I ignore the hand that is slowly inching the hemline of my dress up as the fingers around my leg begin to play with the inner side of my thigh.

'What do you know about John's accident? And what do you mean by a possible murderess?'

My gathered skirt now rests on his wrist, while his fingers stroke the bare flesh above my stocking top.

'I called round hoping to see the book. Unfortunately, things got out of hand. I wasn't convinced when he said he didn't have it. I was trying to get him to tell me where it was, with the help of a little head dunking in the bath. He put up more of a struggle than I thought him capable of. We slipped on the wet floor and he cracked his head on the tap.

'Poor sod was in a bad way. He needed some serious medical treatment, which I couldn't afford him to have. Well, I couldn't implicate myself could I. I hadn't a lot of choice really. He was hurt pretty bad and mightn't have made it to the hospital anyway.

'So I banged his head again in the same spot. When I couldn't find a pulse, I left him there. I added a few touches to make it look more convincing as an accident. I thought my turning the heater on and overturning the stool was quite clever. I've never liked him. And don't think my confessing will do you any good. There was no one around to see me go in or come out, and I parked well away from the house. I was never there. Think about it, Emily.'

There's a lot to think about. I'm the one with the obvious motive. And how do I know that no one saw me in Fitz Park that day? An enquiry could jog someone's memory and put me near the scene of the crime. He's really got the upper hand this time.

A noisy crowd rounds the corner. Phillip's fingers stop caressing the smooth silky material covering my crotch, and he moves away from me.

'Think about it Emily. I'll be in touch.' He tosses me my keys and then moves off in the opposite direction to the revellers, keeping his head down to hide his face.

Chapter 35

My mind replays the conversation with Sergeant Outhwaite several times over the next few days. I already have the motive: the valuable book. I have been told that John's death was no accident. So, if they do have cause to exhume the body, they *will* find two head wounds. No one is likely to suspect Phillip. He's covered his tracks well. I'll be the prime suspect. There's also the threat of violence from Phillip. After what he's told me about head dunking John, I'm sure he would carry out his threats. Finding a way to lawfully claim the book as mine has suddenly become not only difficult but dangerous.

I try to hide my despondency at home, but I can tell that Mother and Peter are concerned. To appease them I accept an invitation to go to the cinema. I have been looking forward to seeing *My Fair Lady* but my mind is not on what I am seeing on the Ritz screen.

We return home afterwards and as Peter inserts the front door key, he finds that the door is unlocked.

'I was last out,' Mother says. 'I could have sworn I locked the door behind me.' Peter holds us back and cautiously enters, switching on the light. We advance into the living room.

'No sign of anything being disturbed here,' Peter says. 'I'll check upstairs.'

'The books in the cabinet have been moved. None of us would have left them looking so untidy,' Mother points out to me. 'And that cupboard door isn't shut properly.'

'A few drawers left open and the airing cupboard door. Someone's been in poking around,' Peter calls down to us. We check all the drawers and cupboards but can find nothing missing.

'Very mysterious. I suppose we should tell the police, but with nothing missing, I doubt if they'd be interested,' Peter says.

I make no comment. I'm in no doubt who the intruder is, and now it appears that my family's at risk. I'll need to do some serious thinking, and soon.

Chapter 36

Two days later I have a plan and phone my friend.

'Hi, Alicia, it's me, Emily. Seeing you the other night brought back some happy memories, but I really have to think about the future. I'm in such a rut, fancy living with my mother at my age. I've no friends here, no social life at all, and Workington is so dead after living in Keswick all those years.'

'About time, if you don't mind me saying so. What have you in mind?'

'I'll have to take things slowly. I've very little money, no car anymore and only a part-time job. I can't really afford a place of my own just yet. At least living with my mother's rent free. Not that I like the idea of cadging off her. I thought I'd catch up with the people I knew in Keswick for a start. Is the rambling club still going?'

'Yes, a few new faces, but a lot of the old crowd's still involved. I go when the mood takes me but it's more for the social activity afterwards than the actual walking bit. Mind you, it's getting towards the end of the season, so not many organised hikes left.'

'Do they still go up Scope End? That was my last hike, Trevor's farewell. I got involved with John after that and stopped going.'

'Yes, Scope End is a favourite. Let me look at my calendar to see what hikes are left. Can you hang on a minute?'

I wait. It is only a minute.

'Here we are, Sunday fifteenth, oh no, that was last Sunday. Twenty-second is Borrowdale and, wait a minute, yes, the last organised hike is Sunday twenty-ninth and it is Scope End. Might have known it, they always finish with a tough one. Why don't we go on that? Most of the members will be going as it's the last one and there'll be an end of season booze up after, so you could catch up with everyone.'

'Great, Alicia, put that in your diary. Emily Peel rides again on the twenty-ninth. Looking forward to it now. I'll call you again next week. I'll get a lift to Keswick and meet you in the Grey Mare car park. Oh, and please don't wait for me if I'm running late. Go with some of the others and I'll see you at the Newlands Church.'

For a good few minutes after Alicia hangs up I stare at the phone. I'd known about the Scope End walk all along. The Club's events for each forthcoming month are listed in the local newspaper. My call to Alicia was simply the first step in my plan to free myself of Phillip.

I've thought it out carefully and convinced myself I can go through with it. I don't want to contemplate the alternative, back to a life of poverty and the everyday struggle to make ends meet. Not when I have the means to live in comfort, the means that Phillip, who has no right, is just as desperate to take from me, and is prepared to send me to gaol for. Or worse, kill me, like he did John.

My plan is audacious and will require a lot of luck but I'm desperate. It's him or me, and I'd rather it was him. Now for step two. I pick up the phone again.

'Phillip Scott, please.'

'Emily, this is he. How nice to hear from you after all this time.'

'It's all right, Phillip, you don't have to cover yourself, there's no one listening in.'

'My, you have got a suspicious mind. What have you decided?'

'I don't have a great deal of choice really, do I? You're holding all the aces, except that I have the trump card. So this is the deal. I won't just give it to you, whatever the consequences, but I'm prepared to sell it and share the proceeds. This is my only chance to make a fresh start. John lost everything we had. I can even forget you killed him. I felt like doing it myself when I first found out, but I'm not given to violence.'

'Wait on, Emily, I didn't set out to kill him; one does what one has to. I never expected him to fight back. He was always such a weakling at school, and I wouldn't want to hurt you unless I had to. You're a sensible young woman. I know we can work this out amicably, to our mutual benefit and perhaps enjoy some pleasurable moments as a bonus.'

'There has to be a few ground rules though, Phillip. I have the book and you have the contacts and experience to sell it discreetly. There'd be too many questions asked at a public auction. However, I want to keep you honest and me alive. What I propose is that we be seen together at a social outing. I want there to be a connection between us. In that way, should I have an accident, you'll be questioned. I know it won't prevent an accident, but it'll require you to arrange it extra carefully and of course I'll be on my guard at all times.'

'Emily. You are a surprise. You are making this a real challenge. You know, you having an accident is not on my agenda. Not if we become partners. So, it's agreed, then?'

'Agreed.'

'Well, let's be seen together socially if that's what you want. It's not only the book I'm interested in. Let's be seen to be very friendly. I sensed that you were not altogether distressed by my attention the other evening. You've probably never had a real man. In fact, I thought you were rather enjoying it.'

Enjoying it? A real man? What a nerve! I was numb from hearing his confession and pinned against Peter's car, so there wasn't much I could do about it.

'We'll see, Phillip. One step at a time. I'm going on the Newlands Ramblers Club hike on Sunday the twenty-ninth and I'd like you to come along. We'll be seen together and we'll be surrounded by people all day, so I'll feel quite safe.'

'Sounds all right, I know some of them. Bought and sold quite a bit of stuff in Keswick over the years. I'm not much of a rambler though. Too busy making money for social pastimes but I have done a bit. It won't be too strenuous will it?

'It needn't be. As it's one of the more challenging rambles, there'll be a shorter walk for those who aren't up to going the full distance. You can turn back with the other lame ducks and skip the steeper part if you're not fit enough.' That should make this 'real man' take the bait, I think. Hope I didn't overdo it.

'Touché! As it happens, Emily Peel, I have some rules of my own to add. Only fair. Can't have it all your own way.'

'I might have known. What do you want to add?'

'I'll come on the hike with you and be the kind attentive eligible bachelor that I am. Let all your friends see us together. You bring the book with you and afterwards we'll spend the evening at a less crowded rendezvous. A little hotel I know, where discretion is assured. I guarantee you'll have my full and undivided attention.'

I have no doubts about that, and once he gets his hands on the book, and has his way with me, I know I'll never hear from him again.

'Like I said, I don't have a lot of choice, and you know it. I'll bring the book, but you don't get it until after the hike. I'll need to think about the hotel. After all, I am a normal healthy young woman who hasn't been with a man for a while.'

'Still playing the tease, eh?'

'I gathered from the other night that you were not without experience. So it might be interesting.'

'We'll leave it at that then. Let me know where to meet you for the hike.'

Chapter 37

I travel to Keswick by bus and walk up Main Street to Cartwrights' where I have arranged to meet Phillip. He pulls up in his Austin Healey sports car shortly after the appointed time, the top down despite the overcast conditions.

'Brought the book?'

'Good morning to you too, Phillip. The book's in a safe place and you'll get it after the hike, as we agreed.'

'All right then, as long as you have it safe. The weather doesn't look promising. Where are we going?'

'Up Scope End.'

'Scope End! That's a bloody mountain. Hardly what I had in mind.'

'You did say you were a real man, and if it will make you feel any better, I've decided to come to the hotel you mentioned to hand over the book.'

The smirk on his face says it all 'Where too now then?'

**

Phillip parks his car outside the Newlands Church and as we walk together to join the group already gathered there, Alicia, who I've seen watch us arrive, catches my eye, shakes her head in a gesture of disapproval and turns her back on me.

An experienced hiker called Desmond is to lead the group today. He motions us to gather round him.

'Thank you all for coming on such a dull day. The weather forecast isn't good but I propose we carry on as planned in case the meteorologists are wrong.'

There is a chorus of, 'Hear hear', and someone adds, 'again', in reference to the weather forecasters.

As we set off alongside the Newlands Beck, towards the Goldscope Mine, I utter a silent prayer that the weather will stay as it is. Any worse will see the walk cancelled, but the overcast conditions suit me fine. We're in the middle of the group, which does not suit my plan, so I decide to play the helpless maiden.

'Don't walk slowly on my account, Phillip. I expect you'll want to be up with the leaders. I'll try and keep up.'

My ploy works. Phillip quickens his pace and we stride side by side up the track, closing in on Desmond who's setting a cracking pace. Though visibility is diminishing the higher we get and the damp grass and moss on the track make it slippery, Desmond doesn't slacken his pace. I look behind to see the group is beginning to grow a long tail of stragglers. I can see that Phillip is already beginning to puff and is red in the face. He too glances behind.

'We have a long tail, I thought they would all be experienced climbers,' he says.

We are close enough for Desmond to overhear and he calls out over his shoulder. 'Experienced social climbers most of them. I'm glad Emily invited you. I hope you join our club. We need more experienced people in it.'

The track circles round the fell before the final steep climb and, as I have anticipated, Desmond holds up his arm, signalling us to halt. As soon as I see Desmond stop and turn round, I grab Phillip's arm and tell him I'm out of breath. He gives me an encouraging pat on the back and stands with his arm around me, which I realise by the way he's puffing is as much to support him as me. I'm beginning to feel nervous. This is the crucial time in my plan.

A thick mist brings visibility down to about three yards where we stand, and the eight walkers who have kept up gather round Desmond.

'It's become worse,' he says. 'I don't think the stragglers will want to go any further, so I suggest at least one of you stay here until they arrive, and those that want to, carry on to the top.'

'Do you think that's wise Desmond?' one of the group asks.

'I respect your experience, Tony, but I for one intend to go on. You know what these mists are like. You can walk through them into bright sunshine. The view from the top will be worth it if it's clear and it's our last hike for the year. Perhaps you can volunteer to stay, Tony? Who wants to come with me to the top?'

Four hands go up, including mine. Phillip looks at me in amazement.

'You really want to go up in this weather?' he says.

'Of course, I've come this far, and Desmond is right when he says that you can walk through these mists into bright sunshine. I've done it.'

'Better count me in then. I'm not letting you out of my sight until I get that book, even up here.'

'OK then. That's six going to the top,' Desmond announces looking at Phillip. 'I assume Emily's hand was up for the two of you, and two, no three, staying below. Let's get on with it. Keep to the right on the way up and keep feeling the fell side and you shouldn't get into any trouble.'

We set off in single file up the narrow winding track, Desmond in the lead, three men following, I am behind them and Phillip makes up the rear. We hug the fell side as suggested, touching it every so often with our hands. I deliberately shorten my stride to allow the gap between the man in front and me to widen. I can hear Phillip closing in on my heels. We make slow progress and a moment of nostalgia grabs me as I begin to picture the view that is today concealed by the mist, looking across towards Robinson. I can also picture the drop over the edge of the track opposite the hollow where Trevor kissed me goodbye. It is the steepest part of the fell.

I know the hollow in the fell side isn't far ahead and pray that the bush is still growing there. I begin to widen my stride now, closing the gap between the man in front and me, and at the same time moving further ahead of Phillip. I can hear the man in front breathing heavily. The track is steep, and I can't see him because of the bend. I lightly scrape my hand along the fell side as I walk, feeling the moss-covered rock. Eventually my fingers feel the soft damp branches of the shrub, and as it comes into view I step through it into the hollow.

I have barely time to turn round when I hear Phillip's footsteps. He treads cautiously, almost slithering along the track. He comes into view, head down, concentrating on the rough ground immediately ahead of him, his hand feeling the fell side, almost leaning on it as he moves.

He draws level and stumbles into the bush, startled to find his probing hand has nothing to lean on. I grab his arm. He gasps in surprise at the unexpected contact. He staggers forward, his head hitting the ledge of rock at the outer edge of the hollow. I push him hard, sending him over the edge into the swirling mist. He doesn't scream, but his startled yelp is probably loud enough for the hikers ahead of us to hear.

I scramble out from my hiding place and resume my ascent, moving as fast as the conditions allow until I catch up to the man immediately in front. He has turned and come back down the track to meet me.

'Everything all right back there?' he asks. 'I thought I heard a yell. Where's your young man?'

'He slipped on the track a little way back. Gave himself a bit of a fright. Don't worry. He's OK. Just twisted his ankle slightly, not a bad sprain. He wanted to sit for a bit and catch his breath.'

'You didn't stay with him?'

'No. He insisted I go on and not fuss over him. He knows I was keen to go right to the summit and doesn't want to spoil my day. He'll catch us up after he's had a breather.'

'Well, if you're sure he's OK, Emily.'

The mist appears to be thinning and minutes later I can just make out another fell in the distance. Shortly we join the others and we stand together at the summit.

'Well, I was almost right. It is clearer up here but unfortunately not clear enough for us to enjoy much of a view,' Desmond says.

We stand silent for a few moments and Desmond scans the group.

'Well done, Emily, but where's that young man of yours?'

'He should have been here by now; I could hear him not far behind me at one time. Those wet bare patches of rock slowed me down,' I reply.

'Yes, they're a danger on a day like this. Perhaps he didn't think it was worth going any further.'

'Well, he had stopped to rest for a bit after slipping and twisting his ankle. Perhaps it was a bit worse than he first thought it was,' adds Bill, the young man who had turned back to check that we were all right.

'Experienced hiker wasn't he?' Harry asks.

'I don't know him all that well but he told me he was,' I say.

'That's it then. I'm sure you'll find him waiting for you at the bottom or else where he stopped to rest. Let's get back,' Desmond says.

He assumes the lead back down and I stay close behind him as we return to the thicker mist. We reach the bottom and I move among the assembled stragglers, most of them sipping hot drinks from the thermos flasks they have brought.

'How was it then, Desmond?' someone enquires.

'A bit thinner on top but not really worth the effort. You were all in the best place. Did that young man who came with Emily come back down?'

They each look around the group. 'We haven't moved since you went up,' Tony says. 'No one came down before you, Desmond, and we couldn't have missed him.'

Desmond looks concerned. 'We couldn't have missed him on the way down either. The path is too narrow.'

'Oh my God, you don't think he slipped and went over the side?' I gasp.

'Now then Emily, don't start thinking the worst just yet. If he did slip over the edge he could be lying injured somewhere. We'll need to report it to the Mountain Rescue people, so they can organise a search. But before that I suggest we, say three of us, form a chain and go back up calling out his name. What is his name Emily?' Desmond asks.

'His name is Phillip,' I tell him, my voice breaking and my hand wiping away a tear. Alicia comes and puts her arm around me.

'Phillip. Thank you, Emily. You, Bill, and you, Harry, your first aid knowledge will come in useful if we locate him.'

'Good thinking, Desmond. Too early to panic yet,' Tony says.

The chosen trio head back up the steep track, linked together by a rope someone has produced.

They can be heard calling out his name but come back down shaking their heads and looking solemn. It is a sombre group that makes its way back down the track to Little Town, where Phillip's disappearance is reported to the police, who notify the Mountain Rescue Team.

By mid-afternoon, the sky is more overcast and the fog has thickened, hampering the rescue attempt. Packed lunches and hot drinks are long finished and it's getting colder. Still, no one is prepared to go home.

Alicia sits with me. 'I didn't like him, as you well know, but I wouldn't have wished this on him. How did you come to bring him along?' she says.

'He's phoned me a couple of times since your party, asking me to go out with him. I told him I wasn't interested at first, and then I thought, why not, no one else is asking me out. So I decided to invite him along here. You know, safety in numbers, until I could see what he was like. I didn't expect anything like this to happen.'

It's almost four o'clock, when someone points in the direction of Scope End, and we observe the Mountain Rescue team making their way round the lower part of the fell. They are carrying a stretcher. I see it is completely covered by a blanket, indicating that Phillip is dead. My eyes fill with genuine tears of remorse. Why did it have to come to this?

The police begin taking statements and I smile, knowing I have sown my seeds well. I have anticipated Detective Sergeant Outhwaite showing a keen interest in the inquest report. I can hear Alicia telling a young constable how Phillip had been asking her friend for a date so I had invited him on the hike. Desmond tells that Phillip was an experienced hiker. A woman tells how friendly Phillip and I appeared to be, he had stood with his arm around me at one time. Tony tells how he had voiced his concern about the conditions and how Desmond had insisted on going to the top, and had embarrassed Phillip into going by pointing out that I wanted to go. Bill tells about him stopping to rest after slipping and twisting his ankle but insisting that I continue because he didn't want to disappoint me.

I am questioned last. A police sergeant approaches me and when I look up, I see it is Sergeant Carter. 'Well, Mrs Peel, we do seem to meet in the most unfortunate circumstances. I hope you're up to answering a few questions? It must have given you quite a shock.'

I nod. 'Yes, Sergeant, it did, but I've had a few hours for it to sink in. I think I can cope with answering questions.'

'I've read my constable's notes, so I've a good idea what happened. I just want you to confirm a few facts. I gather you didn't know the deceased all that well.'

'Not well, but I've known him a long time. He was a friend of my husband's. They were at school together and then were friendly rivals in business. I met up with him again recently at a party and he's asked me out a few times since. I declined his earlier invitations as I hadn't got over my husband's death, but when he asked again this last time I invited him along on this walk. I wish I hadn't now.'

'Yes. That confirms what Alicia Rogers told us. You were ahead of him going up the path to the summit. Did you hear him cry out, or any noise indicating he may have slipped?'

'Well he did slip and twist his ankle slightly at one point. But at that stage we were walking together. He knew how keen I had been to go to the summit, so he insisted that I continue and not fuss over him. He said he'd catch us up after he'd sat and rested for a bit.'

'And after that?'

'No, I heard nothing unusual. I was surprised when he didn't join us at the top. I believe he walked behind me in case I slipped, you know, to protect me. I'm an experienced hiker, although I haven't done any for a while.'

'Thank you, Mrs Peel. That should do it. There'll be a coroner's inquest... as you well know of course,' he smiles, 'but it appears to be an unfortunate accident. Poor old Desmond is taking it badly. Blames himself for insisting on going to the top. I've known him for years. It'll take him a long while to get over it.'

'There is one more thing, Sergeant. Phillip's car's over there. The Austin Healey. Someone'll need to look after it. And I'll have to organise a lift home. My mother will be getting worried. I told her to expect me home by about three. Phillip had promised to drive me home.'

'Don't worry about the car, Mrs Peel. Mr Scott's brother has been notified and is on his way here. One of my constables will take you home. Still living with your mother in Workington, are you?'

'Yes, she's been very good to me since my husband died.'

Chapter 38

It's been three months since Phillip's death. I'm taking advantage of a rare fine day to have my lunch on my favourite park bench, although the view's not as good today, with few leaves on the trees and a greyish tinge to the landscape.

As I chew on my sandwich, my mind goes back to the inquest. I'd had one uneasy moment of regret when I was introduced to Phillip's family, until I remembered Phillip's own words: 'One does what one has to.' I agree with him on that. When it comes to matters of self-preservation, I believe in doing whatever it takes to survive.

I've not heard from Sergeant Outhwaite, nor do I expect to. As far as he's concerned, I've no motive to want Phillip dead. On the contrary, I had a lot to gain. He was an eligible bachelor with a thriving business, quite a good catch for someone in my situation. And wasn't he the one who had pursued me?

I'm now working fulltime for Cartwrights' and have been promoted to assistant manager. My social life is no better. I promised to keep in touch with Alicia but haven't. Keswick now holds too many bad memories.

I've almost given up hope of making money out of the book and am beginning to think it's jinxed.

Chapter 39

It's Friday evening, and I'm heading home after a busy week. It's stocktaking time at Cartwrights'.

I have a sense of déjà vu as I open the front door and hear my mother's voice, followed by that of a man's I don't recognise. I enter the living room and see her and the man seated opposite each other. My mother smiles at me, perhaps 'beams' is more appropriate.

'You have a visitor, Emily.'

The man stands and turns to face me. I struggle to place him at first. It's been eleven years since I last saw him.

'Trevor, what a surprise,' I say.

He is smartly dressed. I take in the dark blue shirt, the lemon sweater and light grey slacks. On some men the sweater would appear effeminate, but not on him. He's still the lanky young man I remember but his lean frame has filled out and his face is tanned.

In contrast, I think about what he's seeing. Mother has only last week suggested I was letting myself go, and she was right. I haven't spent much time on my appearance recently. Too many other things on my mind, and today I'm wearing a plain brown sweater and a fawn skirt several inches longer than fashionable. I haven't washed my hair for three days, and it's in need of a trim.

'Sorry to drop in unannounced like this,' Trevor says. 'I arrived in Keswick this morning and heard about your problems from Alicia. She gave me your address and I came straight here.'

Mother's eyes dart back and forward from Trevor to me. She gives me an encouraging smile, and says, 'I'll go and make us a nice pot of tea, shall I, while you and Trevor catch up?'

She heads for the kitchen without waiting for an answer, mouthing 'he's very nice' behind his back.

I take the seat Mother has vacated. 'So, what have you been up too?' I ask him. Before Trevor can answer, Peter arrives home. I make the introductions.

Mother rejoins us with her pot of tea.

'Trevor was telling me about his travels before you came home, Emily. What an exciting life he has,' Mother volunteers.

'That's nice, Mother. Perhaps you can tell Peter and me, to save Trevor the trouble.'

Trevor smiles.

'No trouble. Since I saw you last, Em, I *have* travelled a lot. I lived in Texas for three years and in the Persian Gulf for two, and I've been living in Perth, Western Australia, since last year.'

Mother looks at me with raised eyebrows, at the familiar shortening of my name.

'Not a lot of skiing or mountain climbing in Perth is there? It's a desert isn't it?' I say.

'None at all. I had to swap my skis for a surfboard.'

'What is it you do, Trevor, that allows you to travel so much?' Peter asks.

'I'm a geologist. I specialise in oil and gas exploration, so I've been working where the oil is.'

I realise I've never asked him what he studied at university.

'Then why are you living in Perth, and what brings you to Keswick?' I ask.

'Oil was discovered in Western Australia last year, at a place called Barrow Island. It's a long way from Perth, but that's where the exploration company has its headquarters and I have a contract with them.

'I'm part of the exploration team. I'm in Keswick because they've discovered oil under the North Sea and it will eventually be brought from a platform out at sea to the Shetland Isles, by an undersea pipeline.

'I was hired as a consultant for the project, so I've been in Aberdeen for the past month. I'm spending a week, starting next Monday, as a consultant on another project proposed for Teeside. So, I hired a car and decided to spend the weekend in Keswick.'

'Makes my job sound a bit boring,' Peter says. 'So you've got to get back to Keswick tonight?'

'I wasn't there long enough to arrange anything. I met Emily's friend in the Grey Mare. We had lunch together and I came straight here afterwards.'

'We have a spare room. It's only a single bed but it's quite comfortable. Why don't you stay with us tonight and go to Keswick in the morning. I'm sure we'd all like to hear more about your adventures,' Peter tells him.

Trevor looks at me. 'Don't worry about the bed. I've slept in some very strange places. What do you think Em? Would you mind?

'Not at all. Tell us all about your adventures, Trevor. I'm sure you have some interesting stories. Tell us about some of the beds you've slept in.'

He grins.

Mother says, 'Emily!'

Peter says, 'That's settled then. Let's open a bottle of wine, or would you prefer beer, Trevor?'

'Whatever you're having. I've had lots of both in some very strange places. I'll tell you about those as well, Em.' This time everyone except me laughs.

I'm pleased Peter has invited him to stay. My confidence has taken a battering recently and I wouldn't have had the nerve.

While the men are outside, Trevor to bring in his suitcase and Peter to look over the hire car, Mother and I prepare dinner.

We have a lovely evening. It takes my mind off my problems for a while and Trevor does tell us some interesting stories.

I lie awake for a long time afterwards, feeling as if a weight has been lifted off my mind, allowing me to think clearly again. I've got myself into such a state over the book that I've lost control of my life. I've tasted success and I can be successful again. People talk about starting over but not many actually do it. Moving house or changing jobs isn't good enough. I'll have to change my life. But I know I'll have to get away from Cumberland and leave all my bad memories behind in order to do it.

Chapter 40

I'm not nearly as confident in the morning but I take the first step towards recovery by taking care with my appearance. I don't want Trevor's final and perhaps lasting impression of me to be that of the frumpy young woman he saw last night.

I haven't wholeheartedly embraced the new mini-skirt fashion, at least not as short as some young women insist on wearing them, but the skirt I choose for today does end a few inches above my knees, to make the most of my long shapely legs. And my sweater is tight enough to show off my breasts. After spending a long time on my hair and taking great care with my make-up, I proceed downstairs to breakfast.

I know right away I have done a good job when I receive a wolf-whistle from Peter and see my mother purse her lips and raise her eyebrows. But Trevor is nowhere in sight. For one dreadful moment I think he has left and it must be showing on my face, because Peter says, 'He's cleaning his car windscreen.'

I am in a light-hearted mood when we begin breakfast but feel decidedly sad at the end, waiting for Trevor to say his goodbyes.

'So, are you going to show me around the town?' he asks.

'Yes, if you want, but it's not leaving you much time for Keswick.'

'Hasn't your mother told you? I'm staying here again tonight and going straight to Teeside tomorrow. I thought you might like to take a drive through the lakes with me this afternoon, in case I've forgotten my way around.'

I can see by his smile that he knows my mother hasn't told me.

I ignore the shops and show him my two schools although there is a new modern Grammar School now on the outskirts of town. We walk the short distance in order to stand before the blocks of flats and I try to explain what the street looked like before, when we lived there. We wander across The Cloffocks and follow the River Derwent to Mill Field. We walk through Curwen Park and up to the Hall, and sit on the bench where I listened to Sergeant Outhwaite.

We sit in silence for a while. A slide show of recent events passes before my eyes.

Trevor interrupts the screening, as if reading my mind.

'You look very sad. This town must have a lot of bad memories for you. You should get away from it and make a fresh start.'

I nod my agreement.

'I will one day soon, but it's easier said than done.'

He reaches for my hand and holds it in both of his.

'Did you ever think of me, after I left? I met your husband once, did he tell you? You weren't married then of course. I came to the shop to say goodbye and to give you my address in New Zealand, but you weren't there and I had to leave that same evening. I've often thought about you, but I knew I wouldn't be coming back to England for a long time, so I never wrote.'

I stare at him for a while.

'No, I'm sorry. I never thought about you. There was always too much going on in my life. You were from another world. Some alien being I had a pleasant encounter with and almost lost my virginity to.'

Although he laughs at this, his face takes on a serious look.

'Come to Australia. This Barrow Island project is going to be big. The exploration company has offered me a good job, which I think I'll accept. It'll mean me living in Perth for a few years. So far, I've spent most of my time up north, near Barrow Island, living rough with a bunch of oil drillers. I've stayed in hotels when I've been in Perth. I hardly know the place, but with this new job I'll be in Perth more and I'll need to find a home. It'd be nice to share one with you.'

My mind's a blank. This is the last thing I expected to hear this morning. Had he told me he had a wife and children, or that the real reason he travelled so much is because he's a vacuum cleaner salesman, I'd have been able to grasp what he'd said easier than this. The shock must be showing on my face. He lets go of my hand.

'I've upset you. I'm sorry. Is there someone else? I've been looking forward to seeing you again since I first arrived in Aberdeen and I've been rehearsing this speech since I heard you were no longer married. I get carried away with my own confidence sometimes and I expect everything to go as I want it. I...'

My upraised hand cuts him off. His words are what I want to hear but I can't bring myself to believe them. I slowly shake my head.

'There is no one else and I'm flattered by your asking me. But why me? You must have met many women on your travels. Why would you want a penniless widow, and one who needs a haircut and a new wardrobe at that?'

He smiles, and I see again the confident young man I was attracted too so long ago. He gives me an exaggerated leer, his eyes dropping to the extent of thigh revealed by my short skirt when I sit down.

'My intentions are not completely honourable. The comely widow sees herself through a mirror. I am looking with my experienced eyes.'

I can't help smiling, but I'm feeling sad.

'If only it were that simple. There is so much about me that you don't know.' He can only see me from the outside. I can't hold the smile. I have so many secrets. Secrets that will go with me to my grave. There is no way I can ever tell him or anyone else the truth about my past. I feel unworthy of him.

'What is it , Em?'

'You make it sound so simple. I'm making slow progress saving to go away and make a new start in England. How could I afford to go to Australia? I know no one there. What if I went and you grew tired of me?'

'First things first, eh? Let's take one step at a time. First step, it would be cheaper for you to go to Australia than to move away in England. You can emigrate. The government will pay to get you out there as part of their 'Populate or perish' policy. Ten pounds is all it would cost you. All you have to do is promise to stay for at least two years, or you'll have to repay your fare there.

'There's plenty of work in Perth. I'd be your sponsor and guarantee your accommodation.

'You once told me you wanted to be a librarian. You could study for that part-time, while working. And if I do grow tired of you, I'll simply send you back on the first available plane.'

'Be serious. You might get tired of me. I mean it, it does happen.'

'So you're going to go through the rest of your life alone, because you're afraid to take another chance? Alicia told me about your husband losing your money. I can appreciate that it would have made you wary of future relationships, but you are an attractive young woman, and smart. You could be anything you set your mind to be. I'd be the one taking the chance. I could be stuck in Perth with a worn out old sheila with psychological problems.'

How can I not be charmed by this man? But I am still apprehensive.

'You said you had been rehearsing this for a while. I've just heard about it now. You can't expect me to decide on the spot. It's too big a step.'

'You're right. But if you're willing to consider it, here's what I suggest we do. I have to leave for

Teeside tomorrow. I'll be there until Thursday. My flight back to Australia is booked for the following Monday. I'll come back to Workington on Thursday and we'll spend the weekend in Manchester. There are Australian Consular Offices there, in a building called Australia House, and you can ask them all the questions you want. You can look at back issues of the Perth newspapers to see the sort of jobs that are available. You could even complete the emigration application on the spot, if you decided to go.'

Dare to dream, I tell myself. Grab the time he has offered to think it through and get used to the idea. It's not going to upset his travel arrangements whatever I decide.

'All right, that sounds good. While you're away I'll break the news to Mother and Peter, to see what they think and I want you to promise to think it over as well, before we go any further. You can...' It's I who am cut off this time, but in the nicest possible way.

He moves nearer, so our thighs touch. His hand reaches behind my neck and he draws my head towards him. His lips caress mine, kissing me gently at first, then firmly. Tongues flicker then probe. My eyes close. Every nerve ending I possess begins to tingle and my heart beats at a maddening pace. I'm only conscious of the feel of his lips on mine, as if all my senses have condensed into this one feeling. I feel light-headed, dizzy. I've never felt this way before. Or perhaps I have, when he kissed me on the mountain, but my mind was full of other things then. Being kissed has always made me feel like a voyeur but now I'm in the moment. I'm present. I feel like a participant.

We move apart, neither of us smiling. The kiss must have affected him too, making us both aware we are no longer the two young people who staggered around the room above the shop that first time, grasping at each other's bodies and clothes before collapsing on the bed. My mind is clear, miraculously free of doubts and fears. We stand up and I take his hands in mine.

'I think it's going to be all right,' I tell him.

We return home for lunch.

Mother has noticed a change in me.

'Have a nice walk dear?' she asks.

It sounds like, 'Tell me all about whatever it is that is making your eyes shine so brightly.'

I smile at her and take my new secret to my bedroom.

Chapter 41

We drive to Keswick in the afternoon and feeling as if I've exorcised my Workington demons that morning I decide to exorcise a few more. We don't speak much, content to be together as we leave the main road at Cockermouth to cut through Lorton and take the scenic Whinlatter Pass route to Keswick. Driving down Main Street, we pass Cartwrights' and the shop where I bought the handbag, which now sits on the car floor by my feet. I direct Trevor past Crosthwaite Place without saying why, not wanting any mention of my marriage to John to intrude on our afternoon together. We drive past my former shop, which now sells hiking and camping equipment, and park by the lake. On a bench near Friar's Crag we sit and gaze out over Derwentwater, which today is ripple free, the smooth surface marred only by the wooded islands scattered on it.

'You look sad again. Perhaps this wasn't such a good idea,' Trevor says.

'No Trevor, I needed to come and I'm pleased you're here with me,' I tell him and mean it.

Returning to the car, we leave Keswick behind and take the Borrowdale Road along the eastern side of the lake. About two miles along, Trevor turns away from the lake to pass through the Ashness gate and climb the steep and narrow old pack horse road. I cover my eyes so as not to look out of the window each time we leave a passing place behind, dreading the thought of having to reverse down the steep gradient should we meet another vehicle coming the other way before we reached the next passing place.

Trevor gives me a cocky grin and says, 'Don't worry. I've got nerves of steel.'

I glance across and sure enough there are no white knuckles gripping the steering wheel. Nerves of steel!

We stop to admire Ashness Bridge and walk a short distance to look at one of the finest views in the country, Derwentwater and Bassenthwaite Lakes with Skiddaw in the background, the famous Surprise View.

No matter how often I visit these places the scenery still fills me with awe. I can see that Trevor too is awestruck.

Trevor breaks the silence.

'I've walked over this area several times but I may never get back here again, so I'm glad to be seeing it with you for what may be my last time.'

Anything I can think of in answer to this seems inadequate, so I simply squeeze his hand.

We return to the car and continue on to Watendlath. We have come here to see the 90 foot Lodore Falls and the tarn known as The Devil's Punchbowl. We reach the junction that enables us to skirt the south-east corner of Derwentwater along the road that runs down Borrowdale, past the huge uniquely balanced 2000 ton Bowder Stone rock, to Rosthwaite.

We finish eating our jam and scones in Borrowdale and head home via the rugged Honister Pass. The road over the pass is well surfaced but very steep and dangerous as it climbs to Honister Hause, a height of 1,190 feet. At one time I'm feeling as if I can look over the Buttermere Fells and see Robinson and Hindscarth on our right. Trevor really is a skilful driver and when I comment on this he says he'll someday tell me about some of the strange vehicles he has driven on some of the even stranger roads. I somehow know that if I go with Trevor I too will not be back here again. I will miss this natural unspoiled countryside, but for all its rugged beauty it has not brought me happiness

We're almost home when I notice a sign on the main road indicating the turn off to the village where my father was born. I've never been there but it's too late now. The mine's permanently closed, along with most of the mines in the area, having proved to be uneconomical. There are only four mines operating where there had once been thirty. One of these is scheduled to close next year with another two years after that. Most of the shafts have been filled in, with the only visible monuments to their existence being a few isolated villages, roadside signs warning of the possibility of subsidence in the area, and the occasional slagheap, and even these are being grassed over. During the latter part of the drive Trevor has been pointing out some of the higher mountains he's climbed but I haven't paid much attention. I'm locked into my own memories. Memories that stay with me all through the evening, but this night, for the first time since I found the book, my sleep is deep and unbroken.

Chapter 42

I wait until Tuesday before telling Peter and Mother that I'm considering migrating to Australia to live with Trevor. I expect some resistance but they've both been impressed with Trevor, and are full of enthusiasm. Mother tells me it's a wonderful opportunity, and as she's only fifty-seven, she's likely to be around for many more years yet, so I shouldn't consider Peter and her in making the decision.

The decision is obviously going to be all mine. I don't know why I'm hesitating other than it appears to be too easy. It's almost the reverse of my previous situation where I had a home, a business and a man in my life one day and lost them all the next. This time I have no home, no future and no man in my life before Trevor comes along and the next day offers me a home, a future and himself.

I'm pleased to find I still have a month's supply of birth control pills and begin taking them again.

Trevor arrives late on Thursday and is pleased with his reception. He does receive one minor setback but Peter and I have pre-planned it.

'It's fortunate that the nearest Australia House is in Manchester,' Peter says. 'Emily's Aunt Jane lives nearby; she may have mentioned her, the one who's in the Salvation Army. We've arranged for you to stay with her. The house is only small but I'm sure you won't mind sleeping on her settee for a couple of nights.'

The look on Trevor's face says it all; this is not what he has in mind. He looks quickly at me, then back to Peter, and the colour comes back to his cheeks when he sees we are both grinning. Mother, of course, is nowhere in sight. She was aware of our trick, but felt that a mother should not be seen to be condoning our mischief.

Trevor and I leave early the next day. Mother wants Jane to meet Trevor, so she and Peter have arranged to spend the weekend in Oldham and we plan to all meet for dinner on Saturday evening. This also allows Trevor to leave for London in his hire car on Sunday and for me to return home with Mother and Peter.

Trevor has booked a room in an expensive hotel, complete with its own small bathroom. After checking in, we set off for Australia House. While I spend time reading the Perth newspapers, Trevor brings the officials up to date on the latest developments in Western Australia. I soon realise that I'm only going through the motions, however, as I can see no reason not to go. I have faith in Trevor and I'm once more confident of my own ability to succeed. I notice Trevor glancing in my direction several times while I read and call him over.

'Do you still want to risk being stuck with a worn out old sheila?' I say.

'Worn out old sheilas are my specialty,' he replies.

'On your head be it then. Where do I get the forms?'

He leans over and kisses me, his face breaking out into a wide smile. But when he straightens up he looks serious. 'You won't regret it, I promise.'

'Go and get the forms,' I say.

**

I know the centre of Manchester quite well through my visits to Aunt Jane, and point out significant places as we wander along hand in hand. After an early dinner and a celebratory bottle of champagne we make our way back to the hotel.

It's only nine o'clock as I close the curtains. Trevor opens his large suitcase and fumbles about as he extracts a few things and I sense that now the time has come for us to be finally on our own, he's a bit nervous. I open my small overnight bag, take out a nightdress and hold it up.

'I'll just go into the bathroom and get undressed.' I say. He confirms his nervousness by nodding in agreement.

I throw the garment onto the bed. 'I'm not a virgin anymore, Trevor.'

We undress each other slowly until we are naked. I draw back the covers and climb into bed, the sheets cool against my back. We kiss, and it is just like the last time, my senses concentrating on the touch of his lips on mine. His knowing hands explore my secret places. My body responds. From somewhere I hear a loud moaning sound, deep and throaty. I think it is him but it may have been me. I am thirty-one years old and thought I had sampled all my emotions but this is something new, and something Dr Kinsey has not prepared me for. I'm no longer in control of my feelings and it feels wonderful.

We make love again in the morning and after aimlessly wandering around the city for a while, come back to the hotel and make love again.

Jane and Bob are both impressed with Trevor the following evening, and he surprises us all by attending their Sunday morning service and demonstrating in the hymn-singing what a fine baritone voice he has.

He leaves for London after lunch, as he says he needs a good night's sleep before tackling the thirty-hour flight home on Monday. He and I hold each other close through the night and say our private goodbyes, but no one appears gloomy as he drives off. We're all convinced it's the start of something, rather than an ending.

My confidence wanes slightly while I await his first letter. And I'm apprehensive when it arrives, fearing it will tell me he has changed his mind about my going, but he's full of enthusiasm. He tells me he's negotiated a three-year contract with his new employers, which includes accommodation. He has moved into a two bedroom flat in the University suburb of Nedlands, which he says is close to the river and only four miles from the city. He adds that I will love it.

My application is approved; I have my interview and my medical and arrange to go. In less than three months, I'll be on a flight to Australia. Time goes very slowly during this period, as I prepare for my new life. I work longer hours to earn more money and work hard at making the most of my appearance. Mother is putting on a brave front, but I can tell she's feeling sad now that the time has finally arrived for us to part. Peter drives us to Carlisle where I catch a train to London and board my flight the following day.

Just before we leave the house, I give my mother my handbag.

'I know you've always admired this handbag, Mother, so it's yours now.'

'But Emily, surely you'll be taking it with you. You never seem to let it out of your sight.'

'No Mother, a lot of things in my life will be changing from now on, and this is only one of them. It has served me well, but I've no further use for it.'

She takes the empty bag, and gives me a hug.

I mean what I say. No more manipulating or scheming. There's no need for me to be in complete control of my life. I'm firmly convinced that everything is pre-ordained, and fate will guide my path from now on.

Epilogue

Three days before my departure for Australia, the friendly conductor on a bus that had just pulled up at a stop on Cockermouth's busy Main Street, moves to assist the elderly woman carrying a small suitcase. As he takes her arm to help her with the step down, he observes she is dressed in a manner more suited to the 1940s, than that which the current fashion decrees. She has on a long coat, which finishes just above her ankles, court shoes with a strap across the instep, and a wide brimmed hat that conceals most of her face, and which is hardly required on such an overcast day.

As the bus moves off, she walks slowly down the wide tree-lined street, pausing every now and then to look in a shop window, as if checking on her appearance. It's market day, so there are plenty of people about and she makes slow progress towards her destination, a late Georgian house and the place where William Wordsworth was born. It's quite dark inside, as she knew it would be, having been there several times before. The house has been altered over the years, so there's not a lot to see but she's only interested in the panelled drawing room, which contains Wordsworth's secretaire and bookshelves holding a small collection of books.

A young man, a volunteer member of the Wordsworth Trust, is the sole occupant. He sits behind a small desk, on which lies a white saucer containing a few silver coins. He's talking into a telephone, having stretched the cord as far as it will go from the wall socket. The old lady places a two-shilling donation alongside the other coins, and although there's a large grandfather clock behind him showing the time as three thirty-five, the young man places his hand over the phone mouthpiece and makes a great show of looking at his wristwatch. 'I'm sorry, Madam, but we close at four o'clock on week days.' His look conveys to her that she's considered to be yet another old lady with nothing better to do than while away a few hours in the small museum.

'That's all right, young man. I wouldn't want to keep you from your phone call. I have to catch the four ten train to Penrith, but before I do, I'd like to donate this book to the Wordsworth Trust. It's been hidden away far too long, and deserves to be on public display.' She places the book, concealed in a Marks & Spencers' wrapping bag, on the table, next to the saucer.

The person on the other end of the phone must have spoken, as the attendant removes his hand, and says, 'Sorry Margaret, someone in the room, won't be a sec.'

Then he turns to the old woman. 'Thank you, Madam; it's very kind of you.' He makes no move towards the book and returns to his phone call. The old woman smiles and walks out of the room.

It's a full fifteen minutes before the young man bursts through the front door. He runs down the short path, through the gate and onto the street, clutching the book, now minus the M & S wrapping. He looks up both sides of the street in search of the old woman, before rushing back to fumble with a bunch of keys and lock the door. After looking at his wristwatch, he sprints across the wide street and sets off in the general direction of the railway station, hoping to get there before the four ten leaves for Penrith.

Further down the street, a smartly dressed young woman, carrying a small suitcase containing her mother's old coat, a pair of court shoes with a strap across the instep, and a wide brimmed hat, is about to board a bus to Workington. She notices the young man with the frantic look on his face, hastening along the pavement, and smiles.

'Goodbye Sergeant Outhwaite, goodbye you accursed book, you're someone else's problem now.'